The JFK Conspiracy: Breakthrough Evidence

by
e. z. friedel, M.D.

Bloomington, IN   Milton Keynes, UK

authorHOUSE®

AuthorHouse™
1663 Liberty Drive, Suite 200
Bloomington, IN 47403
www.authorhouse.com
Phone: 1-800-839-8640

AuthorHouse™ UK Ltd.
500 Avebury Boulevard
Central Milton Keynes, MK9 2BE
www.authorhouse.co.uk
Phone: 08001974150

First published by AuthorHouse 2/20/2007

ISBN: 978-1-4259-9216-3 (sc)

*Printed in the United States of America
Bloomington, Indiana*

This book is printed on acid-free paper.

DEDICATION

To The History Channel, specifically to Nigel Turner and his staff, for their series on the JFK Assassination. The meticulous computer study of the Polaroid negative taken by Mary Moorman at the instant of impact clearly demonstrates the kill shot entering the forehead of President Kennedy. This along with computer studies of several official autopsy photos offer conclusive scientific proof of a conspiracy. The fact that it has taken so very long to get to this point in our understanding of the murder mirrors the enormity of the plot and cover-up.

Even more this work is dedicated to the memory of the victim. President John F. Kennedy was not a perfect man but he was a wonderful leader. His ability to rally the youth of the day was magical. I know because I was proudly one of them. He raised the bar for our nation and the world regarding basic human rights, such as life, liberty, and justice. How tragic that this charismatic figure would die with his rights being abused so badly.

TABLE OF CONTENTS

THE ASSASSINATION

THREE PROFESSIONAL ASSASSINS SITUATED ABOVE AND TO THE REAR OF THE PRESIDENTIAL LIMOSINE FIRE PRIMARILY SMOKE SCREEN ROUNDS AT THE QUARRY. THE MARKSMAN ON THE HILL SENDS HIS BULLET DOWN UPON THE LEADER'S THROAT. THE HITMAN HIDDEN IN THE ELM STREET STORM DRAIN (NORTH) AIMS HIS MISSILE UPWARD, EXPLODING PRESIDENT KENNEDY'S BRAIN. OVERALL, THREE BULLETS STRIKE THEIR TARGET. TWO ENTER FROM THE FRONT. ALL FIVE SNIPERS USE SOPHISTICATED, HIGH POWERED RIFLES. ALL MARKSMEN ESCAPE THROUGH DIFFERENT AND WELL-REHEARSED ROUTES.

CHAPTER ONE

The 26-year-old veteran assassin was working a job in Dallas, Texas. And judging from his nervousness, it had to be a very big job at that. Sal Romano stood behind a wooden picket fence, chest high, looking down the sloping grass hill to the cordoned off three lane highway below. The target run was the 80-yard stretch on Elm Street that lay beneath him. This portion of the thoroughfare, from the Stemmons Freeway sign continuing to the storm drain grate, had been chosen as the location for the crossfire. Hidden below ground, the rain catch basin was marked above by the walking path that led from the Pagoda down to the sidewalk manhole. That sniper's nest and where he presently stood were the key spots. The stately elm trees from which the street was named were in full fall foliage. These, the overhanging branches of the few evergreens, along with the fence, itself, would provide him excellent cover. Sal and his ten-man security team had been there over an hour, nervously smoking cigarettes, milling about in their assigned sites, waiting. Then waiting some more. A few spectators, including a uniformed kid soldier who had minutes before been ordered down the knoll, had taken vantage sites sufficiently below him to be out of his line of fire. Dealy Plaza was quite empty, as per the plan. Still, there was an electric buzz of anticipation from the less than one hundred people present. It was twelve twenty and the parade would soon appear.

Sal wore a standard blue winter weight Dallas police uniform as his disguise. His left cordovan shoe was perched on the bottom rung of the fence, and he used it to slightly raise himself up. Every few moments, he would alternate between this wooden crossbar and stepping back, the passenger side front bumper of the station wagon, which was several inches higher but almost a foot from the fence.

Below him and to his right was his partner, Frank Sturgis, dressed in denim railroad workers' jeans and an unbuttoned red and white striped flannel yard shirt. The faded uniform shirt hung loosely down over his trim waist. Underneath he wore a short sleeve white T-shirt. Sturgis knelt by the right front tire, next to a large leather case which held the sniper rifle. Sturgis' back and the soles of his work shoes faced the passenger side door. A standard yellow hard hat was strapped loosely below his chin.

Both men were partially hidden from view on the parking lot side by three vehicles, two sedans and the beat-up muddy station wagon parked in the middle. The autos had been moved there early Thursday evening in preparation. Sal took a final drag on the Camel, and then flicked the smoldering unfiltered butt over the fence.

To Sal's left, only partially visible as he knelt in the bushes growing up against the Pagoda wall, was a film photographer. He wore a similar police uniform, and held an 8mm. movie camera with a telephoto lens.

A casually dressed camera-man stood next to a large mounted movie camera deep in the bowels of the marble monument on top of the Plaza. Both man and object were completely obscured by the deep shadows created by the overhanging roof of the Pagoda. The camera operator had just finished using the telescopic of the three lenses on the 16mm. camera, which rested on the heavy tripod, to film. Switching to the medium range lens, he again panned the relatively sparse crowd on the opposite side of Elm, continuing down to the overpass. He now aimed the camera back to the corner where Houston Street intersected Elm and held it, ready and still recording.

Two suited lookouts, both clutching walkie-talkies, stood thirty and sixty feet down along the picket fence, moving towards the overpass. Another sentry, dressed in railroad worker clothes, stood on the train tracks at the highest point of the overhanging bridge. At almost the same instant, they each began signaling, pointing their thumbs straight up. "Its time," Sal announced.

Sturgis opened the leather case and in seconds had the high-powered custom rifle fully assembled. He held it up and out, moving it towards Sal's hands.

The middle aged downtown dressmaker, Abraham Zapruter, had just climbed up on the corner stone of the Pagoda. He held his new Bell and Howell 8mm camera with a single telescopic zoom lens. Afraid of heights, his office assistant climbed up next to him to hold him by the waist and help prevent him from falling.

To Zapruter's left, three suited escorts who had been huddled in the four-door navy Ford parked behind the back of the monument forcefully thrust open their doors and started to exit. Seated almost directly below Sal on the Elm street curb, two sentries, one holding a black umbrella, the darker complexioned a two way radio, now stood in readiness. The umbrella clasp was pushed in, ready to give the signal to fire away.

Sal knelt to take his weapon from Sturgis, staying low besides the station wagon. He tightened the supple leather sleeve around his left biceps. Then, he spun around and while gradually standing, took several half steps forward. Bracing his elbow into the V of two adjacent wood pickets, he wedged his big toe against the baseboard of the picket fence. Looking through the scope, the rifle tip did not waver. He followed one of the scout police cars, sighting in as it approached the sign area, then continuing to track it down Elm Street as it moved along.

Sal carefully checked out the plaza. He was already sweating and tense as hell. This would be his last job and undoubtedly the most difficult.

Suddenly, he saw the brace of motorcycle cops make a wide right, heading onto Houston. It kicked in, that instant and familiar wave of icy detachment that told him he was now on autopilot; the liberating state signaling the target was entering the kill zone. He would be ok. He was an experienced professional, with a high body count. He wouldn't miss. He never had.

"Here he comes," announced Sturgis, who had taken a standing position behind and slightly to Sal's left, dropping his striped shirt to his waist. "Get ready."

The customized limousine, top down, flags waving, made the generous left turn onto Elm Street. Sal steadied the muzzle tip, resting the stock against his palm while he balanced the weapon against the sling. He carefully sighted in on the passenger side rear seat of the limousine. The target's thick head of hair was held high as he smiled and waved to the crowd of admirers. The car was going even slower than they had planned for. A good sign.

"Green," called Sturgis, as shots began to reign down from the open windows on the two opposite ends of the Book Depository's sixth floor. Then came a few more from the roof of the Dallas County Records Building. Eight shots in all, but so interposed and rapid, it resounded as if a single cascade. The three elevated shooters, firing frantically, were primarily there to serve as crowd decoys, drawing attention from the actions of the key snipers, Sarti and himself. They were the real stars.

Sal aimed the crosshairs of the scope at the top of the target's heart, slightly to the left of the midline. Before the occupants on the rear seat advanced to the roadside sign, he held his breath and slowly squeezed down on the trigger. One shot was all he was allowed. The rifle went off with a loud retort. An instant before, a shot from the rear had driven into the victim's mid back and his upper body had jerked forward in response. Through the smoke, Sal saw a small bullet hole appear in the front of the target's neck.

Sal took a step back. Out of the corner of his eye he saw the target reappear past the sign. The victim had begun to clutch desperately at his throat, clawing for air, gasping to get oxygen in.

Sal turned and took the first of three steps to the right, running along the fence. He stopped and tossed the rifle back to Sturgis, who had moved behind the station wagon and then the last sedan.

Only then did Sal forcefully exhale, pushing the stale breath from his lungs. His portion of the hit was over and he was now on escape mode. His only goal had become rapidly exiting the area.

Sal wheeled around again. He stopped momentarily to straighten his long sleeve police shirt and tie, to look like a proper cop to the parade viewers. As he took a step to the left, he heard an extremely sharp retort resonate below, so loud it echoed throughout the Plaza. So powerful it seemed to shake the entire hill. The frangible bullet fired by the Corsican Lucien Sarti, crouching in the street level storm drain basin on north Elm, struck. The piercing missile entered the victim's skull above his right eye, exploding out the rear of his brain. Sal would not glance down on this final scene of total destruction for even an instant.

Purposely, he turned his head toward the railroad yard and his guidepost, the North Tower. He began slowly walking northwest across the lot toward this site. With each step he felt a little of the pressure lift. He knew at the same time, Sturgis, obscured by the fence and parked cars, was moving towards the electric post with the just fired rifle.

There were shouts and cursing, and a surreal feeling of suffocating fear. Many of the spectators around Dealy Plaza were still lying on the grass, just beginning to look up. There was a thick smell of gunfire and blood. The limo which had been completely stopped for over five seconds in the middle of Elm now peeled out, leaving a further smell of exhaust fumes and burnt rubber. As the vehicle disappeared under the concrete overhead bridge, a lingering vision of despair and disbelief remained, becoming frozen in time.

Crazed parade goers had begun running about, many up the knoll; mostly back into the area behind the picket fence from where Sal had fired. They were ushered away by the two suited men, wielding badges, and now holding guns.

Sal continued walking, nodding to his three other suited guards as he passed. Each man then turned and start herding that portion of the crowd facing them back towards the parked cars and the knoll, further sealing off Sal's escape route.

Sal knew from the tens of thousands of practice rounds at the desert range, once the rifle was handed off, Sturgis would be carrying the weapon low against his hips. He was now walking several car lengths to the electric post, where the leather toolbox was waiting. Sal could visualize him bending over to take the rifle apart and placing the disassembled parts neatly into the compartments. About now, Sturgis would be standing. Then he, too, would begin his escape, going off in the opposite direction, towards the train tracks and the overpass, carrying the large work satchel at his side.

By the time Sal approached the area near the base of the Tower, about a football field from the picket fence, there seemed to be almost nobody around. Most of the people had migrated down towards the Plaza where there was continuing activity, heightened by a slew of cops racing frantically about.

He began walking east along the first set of tracks he came to. The well-used rails gradually curved along the back edge of the parking lot. He lit a cigarette. Surveying each of the Book Depository's sides as he passed, he had some time to think.

Sturgis should about now be at the overpass tracks, handing the case off to the suited agent, who would then disappear over the opposite side of the bridge embankment. Once the well-dressed man descended to the street, threw the weapon in the backseat of the rental car and drove off, nothing could ever link Sal to the crime.

The shooter on the grassy knoll would quickly dissolve into a ghostly apparition, a blurry vision behind a fence. Any consideration of Sal's involvement in the assassination would be erased by forceful men with official stances and shiny badges. The people not present could only rely on the government's prepared reports, in large amount composed before the event and already being fed to the world news media. Three shots, three bullet casings, one sixth floor book depository window. The average person would never have any idea what led to the success of this complex mission nor how very many men were required. Better for all. Some things were too ugly, even for a professional killer whose neck was on the line.

Sal continued walking slowly along, following the railroad tracks behind the Book Depository lot. From there he proceeded down to Houston Street. A slight swagger now appeared in his gait. The street was empty. He had gotten away.

A muddy '61 Chevy coupe with Jackie Lawrence at the wheel stood by the curb on the opposite side of Houston. The car was standing almost directly across from the Book Building, with the motor running. Sal crossed in front of the vehicle and, reaching the sidewalk, walked over. Opening the passenger door, he got in the front seat. Jackie flicked his half smoked cigarette out the window and the car slowly took off down the block.

"We got him. Great job, Sal," Jackie gushed, his walkie-talkie lying on the seat next to his thigh. He drove along Houston for three blocks, and then made a right turn.

Sal had peeled the uniform shirt off and now threw it in the back. "Yeah, he was jerking around from all the shots, but I managed to catch him in the throat. Then, I was out of there."

"So you didn't see the headshot?" asked the over-weight driver, turning to Sal.

"You kidding? Come on, Jackie. My uncle'd make sure I didn't sit for a month I did anything that stupid."

"Good boy," replied Jackie with a proud smile. "Well, kid. They say it tore our buddy fucker's head away. Fini. End game. So, was it a tough shot?"

"The limo was going so slow, it was easier than the first time you guys took me duck hunting. And a hell of a lot warmer."

"Great, you, well, we just pulled the biggest hit ever." Jackie nodded. "Okay, let's get you back to the safe house so you can start celebrating in style. Me, I ain't going to be finished up for hours yet. Once I drop your lucky ass, I got to drive all the way cross-town. Which, by the way, should be a friggen' nightmare with this here traffic. Mooney needs me to pick him up at CIA headquarters. Fancy-pants got two full floors at the Hilton. Place is so swank they won't even let me in."

Sal leaned over to the driver's side. "Did they make it out of there with the rifle?"

"Long gone, kid." Jackie nodded. "You're officially on easy street. Totally free and clear."

Sal thought for a minute. "Hell, Jackie, something this big. Don't know if any of us can ever be totally free and clear."

Fifteen minutes later, Sal sat on the sofa in the living room of the otherwise empty three story suburban house, watching the early TV news reports. A few minutes after settling in came the stunned Cronkite announcement that President Kennedy was dead. Romano opened a bottle of beer and took a long swig in celebration.

Wallace, Cain and Sturgis came in soon after, followed by the guys on the hill who didn't get collared in the freight. The team from the roof of the Record Building appeared about fifteen minutes later. Milwaukee Phil told the men about Tippit before the TV reporters announced it. So everyone understood there was still a huge problem remaining. Oswald, the unsuspecting scapegoat, had bolted at exactly the wrong time. He was very much alive. The two CIA cops had utterly messed up in their ambush attempt; White, in a panic as neighbors rushed out of their homes, had shot and killed Officer Tippit instead of Agent Oswald, their intended target.

Still, it was over and it was a pretty happy feeling. Especially when Ricky and Sarti finally made it in about an hour later. Sarti had taken his time escaping from the Plaza through the mile long sewer tunnel that led to the Charles River. He acted pissed at himself for putting his first shot through the limo's front windshield, hitting nothing but air and lawn. Still, The

Marseilles Madman took the five hundred forty buck pool, hands down, with his second attempt, which proved to be the definitive kill shot to the forehead.

Sarti, long addicted to heroin, would continue to work for two and a half years before being cut down in a South American bar fight. Sal was through right now. When the Commission, that is the heads of the sixteen major crime families, voted on his compulsory retirement and exile, there wasn't much Sal could do about it. Their edict was written in stone. Disobey and he would be, too.

After the ten days in the safe house, Sal Romano was flown to a seaside villa below Cancun, Mexico where he would remain for the next forty years. He did not set foot on his country's shores, not even to see his only daughter, who was four at the time of this sophisticated but terribly sad ambush.

THE SILENCING OF THE PATSY

ENTRY LEVEL CIA AGENT LEE HARVEY OSWALD WAS SELECTED TO BECOME THE FALL GUY WHO WOULD TAKE FULL BLAME FOR THE COMPLEX PLOT. A PAIR OF DALLAS POLICEMEN, VETERAN J.D.TIPPIT AND NEW RECRUIT ROSCOE WHITE WERE SCHEDULED TO SILENCE OSWALD ALMOST IMMEDIATELY AFTER THE PRESIDENT WAS MOWED DOWN. BUT THEIR AMBUSH IN THE QUIET AREA OF OAK CLIFF FAILS. WHITE SHOOTS HIS PARTNER TIPPIT AND OSWALD ESCAPES TO THE NEARBY MOVIE THEATER WHERE HE IS ARRESTED ONE HALF HOUR LATER. OSWALD IS CHARGED WITH THE MURDER OF OFFICER TIPPIT. THE RESPONSIBILITY FOR KILLING THE 'PATSY' IS HANDED TO CAREER MOBSTER JACK RUBY, WHO IS THE MANAGER OF THE DOWNTOWN STRIP CLUB. HE DOES THE JOB IN THE BASEMENT OF POLICE HEADQUATERS AS THE TV CAMERAS ROLL.

CHAPTER TWO

It was morning, and rather warm for late November. Almost Thanksgiving, the newspaper sprawled on the kitchen table was featuring sales for Christmas. Of course, the major news of the day was President Kennedy's parade through downtown Dallas. Fanfare for the event had been growing over the last four weeks, ever since it was formally announced. It got a lot bigger with the news of Jackie's accompaniment, especially with the women in the county. Whatever their politics, they all seemed to adore her.

Twenty year veteran Police Officer Jefferson Davis Tippit sat at the kitchen table in his police uniform. His jacket hung over the seat opposite him, and over that was slung his holster and 38 revolver. His wife, Carol, stood at the sink, waiting for the muffin to finish toasting. He eyed her nervously.

She brought the bread over and put it on the table in front of him.

J.D. took another swig of coffee, almost gagging from apprehension. He set the cup down. "Carol, honey, we got to talk."

His wife of over ten years put the dishrag in front of her, holding it protectively between her hands. The tone of his voice and the fact that over the last year and a half his absences had become ever more noticeable made her shiver.

"What is it? " She tried to delay, almost like she knew, or at least sensed the coming storm. "Think it'd be better to wait 'till tonight?"

J.D. looked at the clock on the wall and shrugged. "Damn, it's past eight twenty already. Shit, I got to be out of here by eight thirty." He paused, sucking in his breath. "Look, this'll only take a minute. And I just got to get it off of my chest. Right now."

He pushed the paper away, getting ready. He stared up into his wife's eyes. "You'd better sit down, hon." She paused, uncertain. He pushed a chair away from the table with his foot. "Take a seat, sweetie. Please." He nodded to her wooden form. "Probably be better to hear this thing with something under your butt."

Carol sat down in the chair directly in front of him, already starting to bow her head in pain. She held the rag out from her body as if it, in some way, could possibly shield her.

"I want a divorce." He began to stammer. "See, Carol... I'm in love with another woman. I'm sure you could guess this was coming for a while. Yeah, well, look, I'm sorry."

She didn't move. Still, she didn't start crying, either. Carol seemed to be taking the news better than he'd expected. Hell, he had been carrying on a romantic interlude with this really hot, big titted waitress at the barbecue restaurant where he also worked, well moonlighted, for years. But his wife never interfered, not in the whole ten years they'd been married. No secrets. Open end marriage; come home when you want to. And he had a long history of drinking and tom catting with others. No guilt there, either. Hell, she knew what he was like before they got married. Thought she could change him. Big mistake. Dumb broads always thought they could make you over, transform you into some cherry choirboy. Right.

She looked up, trying not to sob. "So what about the kids?"

"It's not that simple." J.D. stopped, taking a deep breath. "See, there's other kids that are also involved here." He seemed almost at a loss for words. "Well," he fumbled nervously. "Shit, what do you want from me? She's already pregnant. Damn it." There, he had said it.

Carol dropped the dishrag, agony freezing her fingers. "Is it yours?" she whimpered, looking up at him.

He couldn't look her in the eyes. Instead, he followed the dishrag fluttering slowly down onto the kitchen floor, landing near his shoes. He looked across the room, becoming tougher, more certain. "Damn right it's mine." He paused for a second. "And I love her."

Carol thrust her fists down on the table and stood. Then she pushed the chair away with her right sole. She turned her back to him. "You and your dirty whores. I just knew it." Her shoulders slumped forward as she started to break down completely. "Oh, Lord Jesus." She sobbed loudly. "What am I going to do? How am I going' to get by?"

J.D. tried to console her, patting her on the shoulders. "I'll still take care of you and the kids. I swear, we're going to have lots of dough. I can absolutely promise you that. Why, I could never just abandon the family." Tippit released a deep sigh. "But I needed to tell the truth, for once in my life."

Carol yanked her shoulders away from his arms. She reared her head up, her anguish turning quickly to anger and then pure hatred. "You slimy son of a bitch! I hope you drop dead." She stormed over to the sink.

He stepped back, looking beyond his wife to the clock. It was eight twenty five. Time to go. Time to start earning that dough, performing his key role in this multi-level operation.

"Look, honey. I got to run. We can talk more about this tonight. You'll see, things won't be so bad." He grabbed his police cap off the table and put one arm through the sleeve of his jacket. "You'll be feeling much better by then. Be a lot less hectic, too." He grabbed his pistol and holster. "You'll have had time to let everything sink in and digest. Pretty soon, you'll see it's the best thing for everyone."

Carol spun around to face him. "Why today, you no good drunken sneak? Lousy liar. Why'd you wait until today?" In one smooth motion she turned, snatched a pot drying on the drain board and hurled it at his head.

He pushed open the screen door and ducked outside. The pot bounced off the wall and rolled harmlessly across the floor.

"Carol, I just needed to finally come clean. Well, 'cause it just may be important. I... No, can't say any more, hon." He moved against the side of the house, where he was blocked from view.

"To who? You and your filthy whore? No good home wreckers! I hope you both rot in hell for all eternity. But especially you, my limp dicked lush."

He crossed the back porch and then proceeded down the steps. He quickly made his way down to the garage.

'Stupid sexless bitch,' J.D. thought. 'Great fucking way to start my day. Shit, biggest day of my whole damn life. Well, I'll just have to go work off some of my frustrations. Maybe kill someone." Tippit gave a slight chuckle. 'Or some two.'

He climbed into his police cruiser, removing his hat and tossing it onto the seat next to him. He went to the glove compartment and took out a flask. 'Yeah, couple of big ones.' He took two long swallows. Then he put the flask back as he licked his gums, still tasting the strong sour whiskey.

Thirty-five minutes later, J.D.Tippit pulled into the parking lot behind the Texas Book Depository in downtown Dallas. He parked near the rear entrance and began looking around.

Officer Roscoe White, wearing a tan raincoat, got out of the old grey Plymouth parked three lanes back behind the delivery trucks. He quickly scanned the area, then walked directly over to the cruiser.

"Hey, partner. How's it hanging'?" White greeted Tippit as he opened the front passenger door. "I slipped the receiver between the rat shit cushions in the back. Hope it works. 'Course we'll still be keeping tabs on our boy with the walkie talkies 'til he makes it to the nest."

They had been patrol partners for only a short time but were also being paid by the CIA for over four years. White was a contract killer for the Agency, basically free lance, drawing government cash closer to ten. But for this caper, he was a cop, having officially joined the force almost two months ago. Most important, White had been his constant ally in the various planning sessions and rifle practices they'd undergone over the last few months. "Oh, and I pulled the radio wires. Don't want that stupid shit listening to any news releases." White chuckled. "Might ruin our little surprise party."

"Just a bit. Beautiful morning," J.D. greeted White.

"Uh-huh," White looked nervously at his wristwatch. "We go in at eleven thirty, sharp. We can lay low in the car until then."

"Let's get some doughnuts." J.D.'s mouth was already dry. He scowled as White looked at him like he was an errant schoolboy. "Well, we want it to look like a regular business day. Besides, what are we doing here? Okay?" White slowly nodded and J.D. started the cruiser up.

"Shit," White complained, "you'd hold up a fucking parade." J.D. pulled the cruiser out, as Roscoe White struggled out of his raincoat. He threw it over the seat into the back. Then sat forward, looking directly at J.D.. "Next thing you'll tell me is you got to stop 'n go pee. Or put on your fucking rag 'cause you're spotting." White fell against his door as Tippit deliberately made a sharp right turn. "What a meathead."

Two blocks away J.D. looked at White, "So, where'd you get the Plymouth?"

"Police lot, where else," White said with a laugh. "One of our older, less obvious vehicles."

Tippit began to laugh with his partner. "Perfect, White. Just perfect. You stole a stolen car from the lot. Well, that place has always been like a general store, anyway. Hey..."

"Yeah, I destroyed all the records." White looked out the window, tightening his lips. "Haven't gotten' this far by being stupid."

"Never said you were," J.D. smiled, slowly bringing the cruiser to a stop. "But you are a thief."

"No shit. Hey, there's no end to my talents." White squeezed his index finger into his palm. "You'll see that today." He looked across.

J.D. had often heard White bragging he had killed over fifty men. Shit, so let him blow his own damn horn. Roscoe was real close to being a psycho, anyway.

J.D. now rolled the cruiser two cars forward so they were directly in front of the doughnut shop. He turned the key and looked over at his passenger. "Told Carol I wanted a divorce. This morning, before I left. Didn't go all that good." He began shaking his head. "But at least I won't have to lead a bullshit double life no more. That shit's over and done with. And I do mean for good."

"Tippit, you are one dumb bastard." White pointed with his index finger. "With one itchy hard on. Your out of control pecker's going to drag your fat ass all the way down. I'm just hoping I can escape without getting dirt on my hands." White got out of the car. Tippit followed.

White, now standing on the sidewalk, walked over to the cop who was just putting his foot up on the curb. "Great start. We're supposed to be leveling the President at twelve thirty, and Oswald forty five minutes later. And you're only concerned with who you're fucking tonight? Say I'm not depending on you." He glared hatefully at his partner. "Look, for the next few hours, could you try to act even slightly professional?" J.D. shrugged in response, then gave White the finger.

The pair walked toward the front door of the shop. J.D. stopped. "Guess you're right." He laid his hand on White's shoulder. "Sorry, partner. Yeah, today's the big day. I can't believe it's taken so long. Planning, getting ready."

"Still..." White whistled in appreciation. "Going to be well worth it. Hundred fifty thou each, once we nail Oswald. That's a lot of pocket green." He pulled open the glass door and held it for him to enter. "After you, bud. Wake you up a lot better than that hundred proof piss you drink."

In ten minutes they were back in the cruiser, eating doughnuts and swilling down coffee. Tippet started coughing. He spit out a large bite of glazed donut. 'Too damn dry'. J.D. went to the glove compartment and took out his flask. He poured a small topper into the cup. Next he offered the flask to White, who shook his head firmly. Tippit nodded to the glove compartment and handed the flask to his partner. White put it back, burying it under some papers.

"Yeah, they want our young agent taken out of this real bad. Muy pronto." J.D. said thoughtfully as he took a sip. "Hey, maybe they'll pay bonuses?"

"Simpleton's worse than you." White snarled angrily. "If that's possible. Need a seasoned hand like me to raise the white flag for stupidity. Going to blow his Swiss cheese brains away."

Tippit frowned, sticking his tongue out. There were pieces of doughnut still adhered and he began scraping them off onto his napkin.

"Please, you're making me sick." White took another quick drink of black coffee. It didn't help.

CHAPTER THREE

J.D. and White knelt on the wooden floor of the sixth floor of the Texas Book Depository. They were in the far corner opposite the elevator shaft and in front of the east window, facing Elm. They had already removed their police shirts. After folding them carefully, they were placed, one on top of the other, on a chair. J.D. checked his watch. It was almost twelve noon. He went back to arranging the shell casings.

White was on his knees beside him, his left tee shirt sleeve rolled up over his shoulder. He stood and began rearranging the big cartons piled on top. Then he took several more practice shots, sighting in on the cars passing down Dealy Plaza.

Lee Oswald walked over. He leaned between the cartons, poking his head through. "Is everything all right?" Oswald asked nervously. "I have to get down to the first floor to take the call from headquarters. It's after noon." Oswald's eyes darted around the room. "And I have to be back up to the lunch room by twelve fifteen. Need anything else?"

"No thanks, Lee," J.D. replied. "We seem to have everything about covered on this side. So, how's Cain's team doing?" Tippit looked towards the opposite end of the building, facing the corner of Houston and Elm.

"They're all set up." Oswald nodded. "Ready to fire."

"And from the two-way, Sarti's already entered the storm tunnel system. What a site! Right in front of the damn limo," J.D. noted, with an admiring nod of his head. "Street level. Just like the doctor ordered."

"Yeah, almost like riding along in the back seat." Oswald managed a tense smile.

"And the Headman is on the right side," added White, lifting his rifle which leaned against the windowsill, and looking down the barrel. "Just like the mayor ordered."

"Greedy bastard screwed up my last pay raise." J.D. leaned over, scanning the knoll with his binoculars. He put the glasses down. "Wouldn't mind taking him out, too. Paint that windy shit's wagon blood red."

"Sorry, men, but I got to go," Oswald interrupted. "Good luck. Just remember you're doing this for your country."

"I think about it all the time, Agent Oswald," White replied, turning his back to the window. "But, hey, thanks. See you later. Now don't forget, get back to your stinking rooming house by one. We don't care how the hell you do it. Grab a cab, bus, any damn thing. Just get back there."

J.D. grabbed Oswald roughly by the shirt. "OK, kid. What's the signal?" he growled.

"Two quick beeps of the cruiser's horn. Two times." Oswald wiped the sweat. "Then I proceed to the bus stop. With my revolver. Stand around for a minute, then take off."

"More than a minute," White shook him angrily. "You dumb fuck. At least two or three, to make sure you're clear and no one's following you. Okay, then what?"

"I walk to the car one block down. It will have the key on the floor," Oswald recited. "I turn on the motor and start to drive. I begin my trip over to Tenth near Patton. I park the vehicle about twenty feet from the curb on the opposite side. I leave the key on the floor and proceed walking slowly up Tenth. Where you pick me up."

"Bingo. Yeah, you'll do just fine, kid." J.D. released his shirt. "Keep your head and remember your orders. Texas Theater at one forty-five. From there, it's out of the country for all of us. With big bucks." Tippit gave him a friendly pat on the cheek. "Now, take the elevator down. Remember to pull the switch to hold it on two."

Oswald shuffled over to the staircase. He greeted 'Milwaukee Phil' who stood on the landing. Then, J.D. and White heard Oswald run down the stairs to the next floor. After a minute, they could hear the freight elevator door slam shut. The whine of the motor began, signaling the descent. He and White playfully punched at each other, laughing as they turned back to the window.

"Should've taken the dumb pigeon out right then," White sneered.

J.D. nodded. "Save us the charade of driving around."

White smiled. "Just drag him out of the trunk and drop him on the cold sidewalk. Nailed his fag ass resisting being dragged from the shitty black and white."

The two-way radio squawked to life. "Twelve minutes to green. Twelve minutes."

J.D. grabbed the radio off the floor.

"Hey, Mr. D's supposed to have that damn seizure right about now." He looked at his watch.

The two-way blared, "D is down. Ambulance to site."

"Good," White winked. "Everything's working like a clock. Should draw all eyes from us and our little target practice."

"Plus keeping the south side of Elm free of any noisy citizens." He smiled to White. "So we don't have to shoot all of them, too."

Several minutes passed as the radio blared out the continual procession of the parade.

Finally, out the window, led by a brace of motorcycle cops, the Presidential limousine came into view. They made the turn onto Elm Street.

J.D. leaned over the windowsill. "There he is! Nice big head. That's right, just keep waving, asshole."

White tightened the thick leather sleeve to his rifle and began sighting to his left. "Come on through, you slick con artist. Last thing you do on earth."

"Okay, get set," J.D. called out, leaning further so he was almost against the window frame. He followed the limousine to right before the sign. "Almost there. The umbrella man is standing," he reported. "It's open," he screamed.

The same voice came over the radio, "Green. Entering Green."

"There he is. Shit!" White was looking through the scope as he slowly pulled the trigger.

As the limousine rolled forward, he heard the sounds of cars and motorcycles and people applauding. White squeezed off two more shots within seven seconds. Other shots came from the opposite sixth floor window and a couple more from above him on the nearby Records' roof. The loud discharges frightened the pigeons from the sills and roof and sent them sailing against the top of the window but also throughout Dealy Plaza. He saw they had scored.

Tippit kept checking through his binoculars. "I think we got him in the back. Might have nailed Connelly, too." Kennedy's skull suddenly exploded like a watermelon. "Holy shit!" The force drove the target clear onto the floor boards.

Now just his right shoe poked out of the vehicle. He was finished. "You see any of that?" J.D. could hear his tone change. "Fuck! Blew his pretty boy head clear off. Holy shit! What a shot!"

Over the two-way radio, in a lower voice, "Eagle is down."

White handed him the still warm rifle. J.D. immediately began to disassemble it. He threw the barrel and stock into a large canvas bag, then looked up. White was still leaning over the window, surveying the grassy knoll and street. J.D. said. "Hey, nice going."

"Yeah, I think I hit him." White exhaled with relief. "And shit, doesn't matter anymore. There's brains scattered all over the roadway. You see our first lady trying to make tracks? Almost nailed her right between her dumb tits."

J.D. finished packing the bag and zipped it up. "Okay, let's get out of here. Lee Harvey Oswald, you're next." He took one step and stopped. "Whoa, we'd better clean up around here. Get that damn butt." He knelt and put the filter in his uniform pants pocket. Damn, he always had this conscience thing. Forget that shit. Just move his ass. He rose.

He and White put on their police shirts and hats. Then they gathered up all their gear and walked rapidly to the sixth floor landing.

CHAPTER FOUR

J.D. and White ran down the same back staircase that 'Milwaukee Phil' had taken just before. They stopped on the fifth floor landing and waited. They could hear shouts and cries coming from the outside windows and fierce running on the staircase.

"Damn, hurry up, Cain." J.D. turned to see Cain and 'Mac' Wallace, carrying a similar canvas bag, running towards them down the stairs. "You dump the shells?"

"Near the rifle." Wallace called, already gasping from the one-flight journey. "Get going, Tippit!"

"Alright, one down. One to go." White brushed against the wall, catching some debris on his police shirt.

"Shit, I hope you cleaned up good around there? Wait." The police veteran stopped, turning back to the top of the landing. "Maybe we should go back and check," J.D. asked, feeling increasingly uncertain. The fears were coming back. The big thing Tippit was frightened of was getting caught sticking out as the dirty cop. Shit, the parade-goers outside would tear him limb from limb.

"You fucking crazy?" White yelled while pulling him by the collar. "Forget it. Our guys'll clean up."

The other two men, dressed in open shirts with sport jackets, joined them moving down the remaining flights of stairs.

White, arriving first, stood on the bottom landing. When Tippit reached the bottom, he grabbed J.D. by the arm. 'Milwaukee Phil,' who had run down first, came over to the pair. Officer Tippit handed off the gun case and felt immediate relief.

"J.D., when we get outside, hold up a second. Make sure I can start the drop car before you take off." White listened to the crowd outside become louder. "Here goes. Let's get the hell out of here."

Roscoe White opened the steel side exit door.

J.D. was the first man out. He took a deep breath of fresh air. He felt better already. He was going to be alright.

All five men quickly entered into the empty rear parking lot. White walked over to the Plymouth. J.D. walked over to the police cruiser. Cain, Wallace and 'Milwaukee Phil', with the two canvas bags, got into the late model Chevy.

They were already leaving the lot when White started the Plymouth up. He headed toward the exit.

J.D. continued to wait, then followed the Plymouth out of the lot.

Both cars proceeded to the Oak Cliff section. They meandered, alternately leading, making sure no one tailed. As they approached North Beckley, White gave a stop hand signal out of the driver's window. After J.D. pulled to the curb, the Plymouth took off down the side block.

White parked the Plymouth a block down from the Roberts rooming house.

J.D. pulled up beside the car and White jumped in next to him. "Shit, Tippit. That pig drives like hearse."

"Well, maybe it is." J.D. smiled as he took off down the block.

At twelve fifty-eight, the police cruiser came to a halt in front of Oswald's rooming house. J.D. checked his watch. "It's almost one o'clock. We're right on time."

"Okay," said White. "Give the little pigeon his fucking signal."

J.D. honked the horn twice, rapidly. Then, again. They both bent over, looking toward the rear window of the house. They could see Oswald behind the curtain. Oswald gave an OK sign, and then disappeared behind the window curtain.

"Okay, he heard us." White turned to Tippit. "Let's move. Next stop, off Tenth so we can setup."

"Yeah, pigeon, your limo's waiting to drive you right smack into our little ambush." J.D. pulled out. He was longing for a drink. "Longest drive of your sorry life, you all out loser."

"Yeah, right into our lair." White laughed, as he removed his police shirt and threw it in the back.

"Geez, White, get that ugly raincoat on, now." He looked at White with a disapproving scowl. "Christ, you stand out like a sore thumb with that white tee shirt. Like some rube college freshman."

"Hey, I'm just a plain-clothes flatfoot," White smiled benignly. Then leaned over and grabbed J.D. by the shoulder. "Your turn. You got the big gun this time. So brace up and get ready."

"Yeah, can't wait to see those sweet innocent eyes as I take him out." J.D. began to angrily shake his head. "All that cockamamie bullshit about the dear red, white and blue. Tell you, buddy, it's making me gag more each time I hear that crap." He continued driving at a brisk pace.

"Well, you're going to get your chance." White slapped the dash above the glove compartment. "Hey, better slow down. Few blocks and we're there."

They proceeded forward. J.D. slowly pulled up to the curb.

"Okay, this is close enough." The rogue cop looked over at the hired assassin and shook his hand. "Good luck, Roscoe. Remember to drop the shell in the bushes to prove he was resisting. I'll be coming up Tenth from Paddock. And we'll have our second victim of the day. One President and one signed and sealed 'loony tunes' lone assassin." J.D. put his right thumb up. "Well, good hunting, my friend."

White looked around to get his bearings. "Okay, I'm getting out. I'll go up Tenth. Then double back."

"Hey, would you please hide the fucking automatic under your raincoat, partner." Officer Tippit pointed with a frown. "You'll wind up giving things away before we even get started."

White opened the door and got out. J.D. watched him rearrange his coat, hiding the cumbersome weapon beneath it. Then White walked over to the bushes on the corner of Patton and Tenth. He tossed the used shell.

White crossed Tenth, starting up the north sidewalk. He continued east toward the Denver corner.

J.D. began waving as he drove the cruiser past him, making a squealing right on Denver.

Three blocks down, Tippit pulled into a small gas station. He checked his watch. Then, he grabbed the two-way radio with his right hand. He tried to relay a message but he heard only static. He threw the two-way down on the seat.

J.D. raced into the gas station office. He dialed the pay phone, now frantic. "This is Raven, Command. How's it going?"

"Oswald's just gotten into car X. He'll be at the site within five minutes. Repeat five to seven minutes."

J.D. slammed the phone down and ran back to the cruiser. He got in and peeled away.

He drove madly down Patton Avenue towards Tenth.

The two-way radio blared, "Suspect has parked. Car X is in position. He is proceeding down east Tenth."

J.D. slowly rolled the patrol car forward while checking Oswald crossing at the corner. Oswald wore a grey storm jacket and with his head held down, his upper torso appeared slightly huddled up. The mark walked quietly but swiftly down the block.

J.D. gave his final report, speaking into the two-way radio, "I have the pigeon in view. Over and out."

He came around the corner and proceeded to drive down the street, stopping directly in front of Oswald.

He parked the cruiser and unsnapped his revolver.

Oswald knelt over in the middle of the sidewalk, putting his hands on his knees. He turned his head to shield his eyes from the sun.

J.D. yelled through the passenger window. "Hey, get over here. Let's go, Lee." The cop began to slide closer to the half open window.

Oswald slowly walked over to the passenger door. "Okay!" Tippit watched him cautiously lean in. "What the hell's up? You're supposed to meet me past Denver."

"Yeah," Tippit replied. Oswald looked extremely suspicious. The suspect's eyes began to dart around. First to the front seat, then into the back, checking. "But there's been a change. Some snoopy old lady in her yard. Come on. Get in. I got to get you to the theater by one forty-five."

Oswald took one step back, his eyes now white with fear. "Yeah, well, I don't think I want..." Oswald took another step back.

J.D.Tippit, Police Officer in Charge, leaned closer toward the passenger window. "Shit, kid. What the fuck's the matter with you? Get the hell in here."

Oswald stood about three feet from the car window. "I heard the radio at Mrs. Robert's." Oswald's eyes were bulging. "Suspect five feet ten, one hundred and fifty pounds..'bout thirty. You're making me out to be the patsy, aren't you?" He started walking backward, like he had just seen the Devil. Understanding, but fearing it was already too late.

Oswald wheeled and turned. J.D. Tippit had to move. He jumped out of the cruiser, holding his revolver down by his side. He came around to the front of the cruiser.

"Hey, kid. Hold it. You're going to fuck up everything."

Oswald screamed, "Get away from me, J.D.." The terrified young man stumbled backward, almost falling down.

Tippit raised his gun. "Freeze, you little shit." J.D. fired a single shot. He missed. It went over Oswald's head. How could this have happened?

Oswald crouched over. His face had drained of color. He took several stumbling steps toward the side of the house behind him.

The gun wouldn't fire, the trigger didn't move forward or backward. Tippit remained holding the base, now trying desperately to pull the jammed lever. In his mind he saw a fluttering dishrag slowly dropping to the floor.

J.D. began slapping the barrel of the gun with his other palm. Desperation was taking over. Then Officer Tippit froze. How could this just keep getting worse? A few neighbors had started to come out of their houses.

From the corner of his eye he saw White approach rapidly from the shadows on the opposite side of Tenth. Oswald was now about thirty feet away. J.D. heard a shot fired behind him and almost immediately felt a heavy sting in his back, like an extremely hard punch.

The veteran police officer spun around to face the barrel of White's gun. J.D. suddenly understood it was his own partner and he had shot him. Tippit saw the gun fire rapidly and, almost simultaneously felt the choking impact of two more bullets tearing into the front of his chest. The pain was excruciating. He couldn't talk and could hardly breathe. What was White doing? Was J.D. going to die right here, on the street?

White walked towards the rear of the cruiser. Tippit had fallen onto his knees. The pain was increasing with no break at all. JD rolled onto his good side, away from the bullet holes and terrible knifing pressure. As he looked up, he saw Oswald still standing, terrified.

"Get going. I'll take care of this," White ordered as he came forward, moving around the open driver's door. "Remember your orders, you stupid Marine? Get to the fucking theater. ASAP! Now, scram."

Tippit heard the patter, Oswald's feet running down between houses. He looked up to see White standing over him, his automatic pistol aimed down at his head, maybe a foot away. He tried to reason but no words came out. He tried to beg but...nothing. He saw White's hand squeeze down upon the trigger and felt an explosion deep within his brain that would not stop.

J.D.Tippit couldn't move. He was instantly paralyzed, his eyes remaining open even as his life rapidly began to leave him. He saw White start to run down Tenth, toward the waiting Plymouth. He heard the screech of peeling tires.

Neighbors came out, crowding about him. He thought he heard one of them say, "Looks dead."

Someone picked up the two-way radio in his cruiser, shouting, "There's been a shooting. It's a police officer. He's been shot."

Then J.D. heard only silence. He felt himself being lifted into a warm, golden tunnel. A feeling of love and forgiveness completely enveloped him. He wasn't angry at Carol. Nor was he pissed at his sixth and last patrol partner. He wasn't even thirsty. He was finally at peace.

CHAPTER FIVE

The sun was already turning down. It was now getting to be late Friday afternoon in Dallas. Five and a half hours earlier, President John Fitzgerald Kennedy had died in a fierce assault. Forty five minutes later, so had Tippit.

Jack Ruby had been busy, first hustling over to Parkland. There he dropped the bullet from the Coccaro rifle on the used stretcher in the hall outside the E.R. Trauma Room. When he had first scurried over to the gurney, he thought for sure it was JFK's. There was an awful lot of blood. But then he had heard two nurse's yakking away as he hurried through the ambulance entrance. Seems that stretcher had most likely been used to haul Governor Connally who was alive and kicking. Jack got a little sick, but he couldn't go back inside. Then, when he heard the news about Tippit on his radio, the cop being killed instead of the target, the lifelong gangster was ready to puke his guts out. Oswald was still alive and out there. Jack had driven back to the Carousel Club in a daze, sensing that these next few days would become the very worst in his whole shitty life.

Now, he sat on the edge of his office desk. To his right, Sam 'Mooney' Giancana leaned over menacingly. To his left was that bloated cow, General Labell, the former CIA Asst. Director. Neither looked all that friendly. He was in this horrible trap. And there was absolutely no way out. White had killed Tippit, instead of White and Tippit killing Oswald. What a total fuck-up. He was screwed, pure and simple.

Giancana, Mafia don and chief architect of the assassination plan, spoke first. "One things for damn sure. We have to do this before the pigeon's transferred out of headquarters."

"So I let him go by at the press conference?" Ruby swallowed, trying to keep the panic from his voice.

"Well," Labell drawled. "At least make sure everyone knows he's a Castro sympathizer, Mr. Fair Play and all. You know the background."

"Pack just in case," Giancana snapped. Ruby had never seen Mooney this tense. The Head of the entire U.S. Crime Syndicate came even closer. "With all them noisy reporters and camera' stooches around, it'll be a lot smarter to nail the pooch in the garage." Giancana stayed almost inches from him, breathing fire.

Labell drifted behind the desk. He wasn't the frightening one. It was Mooney. Always. He remembered back to when Giancana had first earned his nickname: The Justice of the Peace. If anything, Sam had gotten crueler, more deadly. Labell continued to drone, but Ruby was looking squarely in his boss's direction.

"My brother, Earle the mayor, says he can control things so much better down there." Behind him, Labell reached for the blue prints, moved to the front, and rolled them onto the desk. "Including the press boys we like to work with. See," he moved his fat index finger around, pointing here and there on the scale drawing. "There's only one entrance from the street. One back elevator. Two side doors. There is where you come out, Jack. You lay low against this wall and wait. Once the murderer is brought forward from the elevator, you move in. Why, its perfect. Just perfect." Labell had this puffed, bloated laugh, completely false. "We can even set the camera down in exactly the best place."

"So Sunday's the day." Sam poked his finger into Tippit's sweaty chest. "You alright with all of this, Hebe?"

Jack smiled, looking a lot more unsure then he wanted to show. What the hell? No one could deny this was a extremely difficult spot. "Don't have to worry about me, Sam. I'm waiting for my moment in history."

Labell snorted, resembling a pig. A fucking back stabbing CIA pig. "The grief stricken citizens won't ever see how their hot-shot President was gunned down. But they sure as hell will see his crazed lone wolf assassin being eliminated. Step by step." Labell gave the irritating laugh. Looked up, then he did it again. "So Jack, after the press conference, drop by the Captain's Office. My brother, Earle, the mayor, and I want to take you downstairs. Hell, we'll even walk you through the layout. So you're completely set on where you come in and when you start to move towards the suspect. Are we in agreement?"

"Yeah, General. Agreed." Ruby gave Labell an icey stare. "I can't believe those shitheads screwed up so bad. Where the hell you find scum bags that worthless? Really left me holding the bag."

"Well, I must admit we'd all be a whole lot happier if they had eliminated Mr. Oswald, rather than each other." Labell put his hands out. "But when Tippit froze, White had to shoot him. Neighbors, and they are all potential witnesses, were pouring out of their homes, wanting to know what the gunshot noise was about. By then, Mr. Ruby, the cat was, unfortunately out of the bag."

Giancana pointed his index finger directly into Labell's gut. "You can call them CIA. Give them fancy badges. They're still just chicken shit cops, hiding their booze in paper bags."

"Everyone knows most times cops can't shoot straight," Ruby felt so angry he could cry. "But these fucked up clowns couldn't even pull the damn trigger."

"Leaving our boy, Jack, having to go down with the pigeon." Sam shook his head sadly. "Dirty rotten shame." Jack could feel where Sam had put his arm around his back. Now, Sam patted him affectionately. "But Jack's a real pro, right, Jack?"

"Yeah, but I'll never get out. I know that already." He fought to appear brave. But Jack knew the score. "I'll never see another free day as long as I live." The second he pulled the trigger, Jack Ruby was sentencing himself to a lifetime in the big house. There wouldn't be a prayer of a parole. "Only way I'm leaving is in a hearse."

"Hey, you slippery kike." Mooney Giancana suddenly grabbed him by the throat and was choking the air out of him. "You knew that going in. And I made sure of it, so there's no excuses now. You have to do this. And you'll do it this Sunday when we tell you. As long as the pigeon's around, no ones safe. He spills his guts, we all go down. This is your job until it's completed. Or you're dead-meat." Mooney released him, and Jack gasped to breath. He leaned over the desk and moved air in and out. Slowly.

When he no longer felt like he was going to pass out, he nodded to Mooney. "I'll show the world a Jew has guts."

"Yeah, Hebe." Mooney smiled encouragement. "You'll be a lasting hero. How many millions of red-blooded patriots would give their right nut to be in you're exact shoes? He killed your favorite president. And the intense grief just overwhelmed you. Case of temporary insanity if I ever heard one."

"And, of course," Labell stood and started to roll up the blueprints. "You wanted to save the widow Jacky from suffering the anguish of a heart wrenching trial, poor dear." He looked up.

"We'd like you to stop down to the Western Union office about an hour before we initiate the transfer." Labell eyes and pouting face reminded Ruby of one of those old time Hitler posters. "We have someone working there. He'll give you an alibi so you don't look too anxious. Can't appear to have been planning this act of rage. Also helps get the police off the hook. You slipped through very tight security. "

"So tight they're leading you from the back stair case straight into Oswald." Mooney smiled. "You just got to squeeze the fucking trigger on your 45. Son-of-bitch gun'll do the rest." Ruby, himself, had heard Mooney say that statement maybe ten times. But this time it was like he was issuing himself an iron clad life sentence. It was his neck, and no one else's.

"Agreed?" Ruby nodded in response to Labell's question. "Good, I'll get back to police headquarters, and give my brother, Earle, the mayor, the green light. We can start to coordinate things with Central Control."

Giancana walked Labell to the door which opened to the front room.

"I know Jack'll do the right thing." Labell grunted, as he pointed to Sam. "But he's your man. So its your neck, if he louses up." He put glancing pressure on Sam's shoulder and held it. "Don't test our tolerance for failure."

"Hey, genius." Mooney grabbed Labell's index and long fingers and twisted them roughly back. "Its all our necks if he fails. And don't start forgetting why we're in this sticky situation in the first place. 'Cause you picked a couple clowns who couldn't hold up your fucking end of things. We're bailing your fat ass out. So don't start acting rude. Or superior."

"Mr. Giancana, just make sure you do." Labell pulled his hand away. "Our President has just inherited the most difficult job in the entire world. And he's anxious to move on to less emotional issues."

"Like your little skirmish in Southeast Asia?" Giancana paused to empathize. "Lot safer shooting gooks than one of your prized glamour pusses. Even if this particular star turns out to be a hopped up double dealing party pooch. Anything for a laugh."

"Let me assure you, the Agency's wrath is not to be taken lightly. J.Edgar Hoover is not a man to be joked with." Labell glowered, not coming even close to creating fear in this crude, uneducated alley cat. He was foolish for trying. "But the most dangerous by far to your organization is our new President. Why, President Johnson will pull out all the stops, you screw him up on this thing."

"Well, thanks for the warning, General." Giancana was at Labell's throat and this time he was squeezing down like he had previously done to his own soldier. "Now, listen to me one fucking minute. We got lots of shit on that cowboy sleaze ball, including the murder of his own sister. On Christmas, no less. And plenty 'bout the Bobby Baker and Billy Sol Estes band of skimmers." Giancana released Labell, pushing him back. "No, we're doing this 'cause we honor our commitments. Even if we go down or wind up in the can. You privledged college grads head for the exit second things start getting rough. Lie. Try to change the fucking deal." Mooney pressed forward. "And, speaking of exits, when the hell are we getting paid? See, we might of even done this for free. 'Cause we love this country easily as much as you hypocrites. But this little caper seems to have gotten more complicated by the minute."

"We'll pay you once Oswald is taken care of. Hundred thou for each of your boys, including Mr. Rubenstein, and three million to you.

"One thing, you've always been good on the cash end." Giancana looked at Labell with pure contempt. "'Course its not like its your dough or anything. You guys have a field day with your hand in the company till. More like two fists. But still, how all you cocksuckers line your pockets can't be my problem."

"You men don't pay taxes," came Labell's brusque response.

"Hey, neither do you, hotshot." Mooney Giancana reminded Labell with a final shove. "Or your lousy politician friends. 'Sides, you guys sell a lot more illegal shit in a year than we can in our entire lifetimes. And we're considered public menaces. If the taxpayers knew the real deal, they'd close you down for keeps."

Labell left quickly, clearly irked. Meanwhile Jack Ruby had walked over to a bookshelf and was looking at some of the old pictures. His mother, old, stooped. Several of his dogs, a few long dead. Tears began flowing down his cheeks.

Giancana went over to him. "Sorry, Hebe." Sam shrugged. "It's a bum deal, alright. Real fucking ballbuster. I know how much it sucks. But its your responsibility. And you're gone to do it just right." Sam Giancana started rubbing Ruby's back with both his palms.

"I'm supposed to be tough, Sam. I've always been a man willing to take his lumps." He turned to face Giancana. "But I'm afraid I'll never see my family again."

"Oh, you'll see them lots." Sam had this friendly smile, like the old days, when he was Capone's free spirited wheelman on the streets. "Hell, being in stir's not so bad. Especially when we're looking out for you." Sam winked. "Lots of fresh young meat. Especially for a connoisseur like yourself. Some real grade A tight ass."

"I've had this bad cough." Ruby felt the pain deep in his chest. It had been going on over a year, now. But recently, he had begun getting this sudden shortness of breath with it. "The doctor thinks I may have a tumor."

"Sorry to hear that, paisan." Giancana looked sincerely sorry. "So what the fuck? You'll go out in a blaze of glory. National TV. Taking out the bad guy. Lot worse ways to go."

"It's all happening a bit too fast." Jack nodded, giving a small flicker of a smile. "But I'll be all right."

"Course you will, Hebe. Hell, some cutie's pecker pounding your sphincter's got to be lots more appetizing than an electric cattle prod."

This time it didn't sound like a threat. Maybe Mooney was just trying to cheer him up. Well, it sure was better than being tortured to death. Ruby still remembered Action Jackson's ordeal. Anyone seeing the pictures remembered. Wasn't pretty. Three days of severe torture 'till Action had begged them to kill him.

"I'll show all those chicken shits how tough a Jew can be." Ruby looked in the mirror, and made fists with both hands.

"Yeah, Jack. Like the old days when you guys nailed Christ. And Goliath, he had to be one tough motherfucker. Took his fat ass out with a hand-made slingshot." Giancana gave a him a playful swipe near the jaw. "No five and dime stuff for you guys."

"We didn't do Christ." Ruby protested. "He got fucked by the Romans, same as us." Jack was thinking same as me. Fucking anti-Semites. Lot of Jew haters through the ages. Everyone always needs a hanging boy. Just like now.

"So somethings never change." Mooney shook his head in agreement. "Just show 'em your balls,

Jack. In a couple years, when everything dies down, you can stroll out on a wacko plea. Day of your release, I'll make sure you're made. That's a solemn promise." Sam 'Mooney' Giancana made the sign of the cross. "And shit, we didn't do that for your bagle bending tribesman Lansky."

"Thanks, Sam." He couldn't believe his ears. He was being given a higher send off rank than even Meyer Lansky, the brains of the whole worldwide Outfit. The smartest Jew in the roughest, toughest business ever was kept out. "That means an awful lot to me."

"Don't mention it, kid. And Jack, you can start calling me Mooney. You're one of my real heroes. You, Joe Dimaggio, and Al Capone. All big hitters." Mooney paused, shaking his head in admiration. "But shit, you're a lot tougher than Joltin' Joe. He quit the second he got a little pain in his foot. My man Mr. Rubenstein's just getting started." Giancana suddenly turned deathly serious. He pointed to Ruby's right side. "Oh, Jack. Make sure you aim for his liver. I seen a lotta heart shots miss.

THE PRESIDENTIAL AUTOPSY

THREE GUNSHOT WOUNDS, TWO FROM THE FRONT, ARE CHANGED BEFORE THE OFFICIAL FORENSIC STUDY BEGINS. THEY SOON BECOME TWO ARTIFICIAL ONES FROM THE REAR. THIS IS DONE BY A COVERT TEAM SPECIFICALLY TRAINED FOR THIS MISSION. THE NEW FINDINGS BECOME THE KEY EVIDENCE FOR THE IMMEDIATE AND FINAL CONCLUSION, THAT THERE HAD BEEN ONE, AND ONLY ONE, SHOOTER. IN LESS THAN TWENTY-FOUR HOURS, THE LONE ASSASSIN HAD BECOME A PERMANENT PART OF AMERICAN HISTORY AND LEE OSWALD WAS CAST AS ONE OF ITS GREAT VILLIANS. THE INVESTIGATION WAS OVER BEFORE IT HAD BEGUN.

CHAPTER SIX

The Army helicopter, which had just arrived from Walter Reed, was already hovering well above its landing site when Air Force One hit the ground at Andrews Air Force Base in Prince George's County, Maryland. Captain Riddel, his name plate on his front jacket pocket, his gold bars on his starched shirt lapels, waited anxiously. He was plenty nervous and there was a tightness in the pit of his stomach he had never felt.

Seated on the back seat of the helicopter, he leaned anxiously over the pilot's shoulder, staring out at the tarmac. His code book, a red TOP SECRET emblazoned across the front and back laminated black covers, sat in his lap. His knees bounced up and down.

"Take her down to about ten feet." He pointed with his thumb. "We'll wait there."

"Yes, sir," replied the young helicopter pilot. The helicopter gently lowered, the craft now holding her position.

Riddel pushed the pilot in the back. "But keep everything going at full ready. We'll want to make a quick departure back." Time was of the essence.

From the radio in front of the pilot came a blaring report. "Air Force One has landed. Proceeding to unloading area."

He looked around nervously. "Once we get the body, of course." Riddel, in his early forties turned to General Weiss, longtime Chief of Neurosurgery at Walter Reed Army Hospital in Silver Spring. "Ready, General?"

The General gave a slight smile. "Of course, Captain."

Captain Riddel didn't like his attitude. Not one bit. They had met only three times before tonight and the old timer had just been informed of his new role a couple of hours before. Still, he'd better straighten the codger out right now. "Don't forget, on this mission I'm Designated Commander." He pulled at the General's sleeve. "You take orders from me. So stop thinking and do exactly as you're told. Remember, this is a defining moment in our great nation's history." He nervously glanced at his watch. "And we've got precious little time to pull it off. Everyone at Central Command is depending on your medical expertise. Quickly and concisely, mind you."

The tower announced, "Have ambulance ready on left port. No, make that rear. Did everyone get that? Rear hatch on Air Force One."

There was another squawk from the radio, "Roger, tower. Loading dock apparatus already in place."

He looked out the helicopter window to view Air Force One taxiing in, directly to the left front of him.

"Well, here it comes. The big bird. With our bullet riddled cadaver." He took an excited breath.

"Should be one hell of a challenge." He turned back to the pilot. "Take the craft down."

Air Force One taxied past the now grounded helicopter. He lost sight of it as the plane made a gentle left turn.

Shortly after, the large plane reappeared. It slowly rolled into the runway area directly in front of the helicopter, blocking the view of the newsmen and dignitaries waiting mournfully near the ambulance. The helicopter was now completely hidden behind the bigger airship.

It was time. "Open the back hatch," Captain Riddel ordered.

The helicopter co-pilot slid open the door to the back seat and rear compartment directly behind and to his right. He felt the cool breeze from the early night air.

The airman flipped down the steel ladder. The heavy thrust of the fully idling rotors above them shook the cabin forcefully. He heard the sound of the metal edges dragging onto the asphalt.

Air Force One stopped directly in front of them. There was a sudden calm as the jet engines went silent.

The large heavily mounted t.v. camera moved into the area of the rear compartment of the huge plane, which was just now opening. First the camera followed Attorney General Robert Kennedy racing up the portable steps that had already been attached to the front passenger door. He disappeared into the plane. Then the camera focused in on the now opened rear compartment revealing the heavy ornate bronze coffin being lifted up by a group of older suited men.

Riddel peered out his side window. Directly in front of the helicopter, the galley door to Air Force One swung open.

Quickly, two sergeants on the ground locked a portable stair assembly onto the plane at the right front portal. Almost as if on signal, a thin, well-built man in his late forties appeared in the galley doorway. From the way he was struggling, buttocks first, legs set widely apart, it was obvious he was carrying something heavy. He used his whole left side as he kept driving his hip under the mass to support it. At the same time, he continued pulling backward. The slate grey mass-trauma body bag was bunched near the other end. This end contained the shoeless, bare legs of John Fitzgerald Kennedy, the thirty-fifth President of the United States and fourth to be assassinated while in office.

A heavy-set man in a jacket and raincoat carried the mid torso on his right hip, with both hands clutching at the waist and pelvic area of the body.

The head end flopped backward as an older, frail agent who was in the rear came into view. He tried to support his portion of the body by lifting the corpse's shoulders above his waist.

Still, as the other two Secret Service men began their climb down, the back end of the bodybag struck the metal grating that made up the rectangular platform above the first step.

"Oh no!" Horrified, Riddel watched this procession begin its descent down the portable stairs to the ground below. The back end seemed to have almost struck again. "What the hell are they doing with my head? That's the most important part. Holy shit."

The men reached the bottom. Suddenly the frail agent let his end totally fall onto the asphalt. "Stop them, someone. Those clumsy idiots are about to dribble our head down the tarmac." Riddel pushed the co-pilot's shoulder. "Get out there. And support the fucking thing before it falls off, Sergeant. Cradle the ears and neck like you would a newborn baby. And hold it above the body, for Christ's sake. Think of it as a thin porcelain egg. Go."

As the co-pilot jumped out, Riddel turned to the General. "We should have practiced this part, also. Who would have thought they could be this incompetent?" His eyes reflected his anger and dismay. Then, he stared into the General's hazy blue eyes. "Okay, you can get in the back.

And take your damn jacket off, General. Put that apron on. Wait!" He grabbed him by the elbow. "When you go back, toss me mine. This could get bloody in a hurry."

"Well, we're not going to start the dissection here, are we?" the General looked at him with growing apprehension.

"And why the hell not? Says in the damn code book," Riddel lifted the book off his lap. "Right here." He tapped at the spot. "In fucking big block letters. Page two. Item 3. 'All ammunition fragments should be removed as quickly as possible.' Well, I'll bet our body's just loaded. And we've got less than a half hour to make everything look right. When the First Lady reaches the Naval Hospital, we have to be just about finished. And everything has to look reasonably tight."

"But still," the General had an agonized look on his face. "Shouldn't we do this in a more controlled setting?"

"Listen, you senile son of a bitch." Riddel grabbed at the General's jacket. "This is a controlled setting. We're alone, right?" He pushed the older man roughly. "You know for being the Head of Neurosurgery at Reed, you're sure not very sharp. Or resourceful. You got to start thinking outside the box on this one. Now get the hell in the back, please." He pointed at Weiss, glaring. "And put some damn gloves on. At least look like you're ready to do this thing."

The Captain turned back to look outside his left window at the procession. He watched the co-pilot run over and push aside the older agent as he grabbed the head. In doing this, the elderly man lost hold of the right shoulder and the entire upper body twisted awkwardly downward, almost hitting the gravel ground cover. "Holy shit. Tell me I didn't just see that." The four men struggled to each grab hold of a part of the bag to hold it up.

"What the hell are those clods doing now?" He shuddered. "Get both the shoulders up, you stupid shits." They seemed to get control and begin proceeding back. "OK. That's better."

The General reappeared, and approached to stand behind the Captain's shoulder. He placed the surgical apron onto the empty seat.

"Look what those jerks are doing to our body," Riddel agonized. "Total incompetents."

The General leaned over Riddel's shoulder, looking out the same window. "Well, they seem to have it now. Here they come."

The procession continued over to the opposite side of the helicopter.

"Okay, let's get the damn body into the back. Here, help me take off my jacket." The General did as he was asked, holding one of the Captain's sleeves. The Captain then tossed his jacket onto the seat on top of the apron. He stood, turning. He nervously cracked his knuckles as he grabbed for the apron, managing to edge a sleeve of the jacket down onto the helicopter floor. He tied the apron as he proceeded into the rear of the plane.

The co-pilot's head was the first to appear in the doorway.

"Here, let me give you a hand," volunteered the pilot, stepping into the back. The head end of the bag appeared first. Then the oldest agent's head and shoulders appeared holding the mid part of the cadaver.

The rest of the slate grey body bag now appeared as they managed to lift it onto the floor. The two other men stood on the ladder in the doorway.

Then, they began to slide the corpse to the rear. The body bag, burdened down with its human weight, caught the hem of the jacket arm as it slid past.

As the two agents climbed in to push at the feet, the bag slid forward, dragging the jacket beneath it.

They continued inching the body bag backward to the area in the rear where several large lights were shining brightly down onto the floor.

Riddel checked the progress, then went to the bottom draw of a large metal cabinet secured against the back wall. He removed a large, Army green instrument tray, circled with a single tie. He pulled the knot out. He then spread the major surgical instruments out. There were several instruments added. Adson forceps, a few micro hemostats, a microtome, like what the hell would they ever need to be using something like that. He smiled, remembering his heated discussion when they had gone over creating this tray. He had been right, naturally enough. Kept saying 'forget the finery, just big and strong.'

The helicopter door slammed shut.

"Let's go, pilot," Riddel ordered. Almost immediately, the nose of the plane tilted as the helicopter began its swift ascent. The plane climbed back toward the east gate and away from Air Force One and the crowd of people gathered.

The elaborate bronze coffin was now being lifted down to the tarmac by a large group of individuals in suits at the rear of the plane. Mrs. Kennedy and RFK followed.

The Captain viewed this throng through the rear view mirror. "Okay, get us to Reed. And stay on it." The Captain turned to the suited men. "Drag the head in over the lights. And open that bag." The men went over and lifted the body forward. "But don't take him out of it. We'll work right as it is."

The agents unzipped the bag, revealing the upper torso of the late President. John Fitzgerald Kennedy's head was wrapped in a large bloody sheet that went around his crumbled head almost twice.

"And get that damn sheet off," he ordered. The agents began to quickly unwrap the covering. "Be gentle, dammit. You've got a human head in there."

The sheet was unwrapped and allowed to lay beneath him. There was a huge area of destruction that constituted the upper front and right side of the President's head. Clots and serous exudate poured out from both the front and rear exit wound, which was at least fist sized.

There was a burnt entrance wound the size of a quarter in the high temple area about five inches above and slightly to the right of the right eye socket. The eyebrow and a portion of his sideburn were missing, with traces of burnt singe marks in the area remaining. A large portion of the curved upper fold of the right ear had been totally blown away. The President's thick matted hair lay in oily clumps with large clots seeping through the various strands. A portion of his hairline, starting at the front temple and continuing to behind the damaged ear, had been torn away. A huge flap of scalp came forward to rest over the right upper cheek.

There was a two-finger entry wound in the middle of John Kennedy's throat. The burnt edges circled outward, revealing a portion of the trachea had been blown away. The glint of silvery bullet fragments reflected the strong light from the overhead lamps. The edges on either side had been extended a few centimeters. That portion of the skin was clean.

The Captain turned the head to the left side. Now, in profile, the full extent of the head shot was able to be appreciated. The entire right back portion of the corpse's skull had been blown completely away. There was a fist size hole in the center of this rear area. Huge fragments of bone with spiked edges radiated outward from this central area of the wound.

Riddel took a single gloved index finger and pushed inward. Almost the entire right side of the skull moved in, as the sound of crepitant bone grating against itself echoed against the metal walls and floor of the helicopter.

The sleek folded jelly-like cerebellum at the base of the brain, its wet smooth membrane giving it the appearance of a huge snail, poked through the back wall of the skull.

The General gasped audibly as did the other men. "My Lord. Looks like he was hit with a bazooka," he exclaimed.

"Frangible bullet, if you ask me," replied the Captain, in an all knowing manner.

"Why, I haven't seen damage like this since my days in Korea." The General's face looked terribly shaken. "And those were bad times. We didn't have the portable field set ups we do now. Or helicopter pick up. Whole different ballgame."

"Yeah, well thanks for the trip down memory lane, General. Now, let's get cutting." Riddel flipped his black top secret book to his side. Then he used the tip of his shoe to nudge the round brown plastic container over to the head area. He bent over the head wound. "Shit, the whole head is loaded with shrapnel. We have to get it all out."

"And then you have the entry wound in the throat to deal with", noted Weiss.

"They wanted him dead. And made sure of that." Riddel's nervous laugh was tinged with dismay. "Sons of bitches didn't give a thought to making our problems any easier."

"Well, we'd better get to it, then." The General replied.

"Here," the Captain pointed with the pick ups he'd grabbed from the tray. "Excise that area for starters. Then we'll see what we got."

The General bent forward, beginning to cut above the lemon-sized area of cerebellum that dangled in front of him. After a few snips, he paused. "Don't want to take the full cerebellum?" The old surgeon looked up. "Do we?"

The Captain pulled the General's elbow impatiently. "Of course, take the whole thing. What the hell are you doing? This isn't some fancy micro-dissection." He stared angrily at the General. "Get the damn brain out, this instant."

The General shook his head, then began making a larger cut along the base.

"And get some decent scissors, for Christ sake. That pair wouldn't cut a nipple, much less lop a whole tit." He scanned the instrument tray. Then he picked up the largest, heaviest pair. "Here, use these." Riddel tossed the scissors down in front of the General on the body's chest.

"Three and a half minutes until we reach Walter Reed," remarked the pilot, looking out his front window.

"Okay, pilot. Just do your job." He snapped. "And we'll do ours."

The General had excised almost the entire section and held it out. Riddel grabbed it and tossed it onto the lid of the round basin.

Then the Captain leaned forward, probing with his right index finger along the head of the President. "Shit, there's no strength to his skull. We'll have to rebuild that whole damn area. Well, forget it for now. We can do that later." Riddel looked desperately back into the cavity. "Would you` get the fucking brain out! Are you blind? There are still large areas with fragments."

The General began grabbing some tissue in the middle portion, and cutting it away.

"Yeah," Riddel nodded his approval. "That's it. Get all of that crap out of there."

The Captain continued to palpate with his index finger along the side of the skull. "You get a chance to look at the throat wound?"

"Yeah, pretty gruesome." The General shook his head again. "That alone would've probably killed him."

"No, I meant did you see any bullet shrapnel, you moron? I thought I saw something glistening in the bottom." Riddel stopped, staring coldly at the General. "Just what in the hell's the matter with you? Retrieve the ammunition fragments as best you can. And as quickly as you can. Even you should understand that, General." He looked down.

The General was halfway finished completing his cut across the tissue. "And that's what you've been dissecting, you useless relic? We simply don't have time, you ignoramus!"

Exasperated, Riddel tossed the General aside, elbowing him in the chest. "Out of my way, this instant. Our country's rep is ready to go down for the last G-ddamn time and you're jerking off on the shoreline. I need it out, now!"

Riddel knelt down, his knees on either side of the head. He thrust his hands around the outer borders of the fragmented bone, then slid them down toward the bottom of the cavity. About halfway down he began wiggling his fingers frantically around the torn insides, tearing away at the thick fibrous tissue anchoring the base. "Here! Hold this up, you idiot," the Captain ordered, nodding to the huge superior surface of the remaining brain. "I need some traction on this baby."

Then he began to squeeze the tips of his fingers towards each other forcefully. They were almost together, when Riddel stiffened his body and made a leap upwards onto his feet, yanking a full two-thirds of the brain out from the destroyed skull. He could only lift it about six inches from the body as the five inch wide rope-thick area at the take-off of the central nerve cord tethered it down at its base. He stared at it scornfully.

"Cut that damn cord, you frozen pussy." He ordered the General as he began twisting the brain on itself. "Nothing happens until then."

General Weiss had taken two steps back. His color had totally faded and his eyes bulged out. "I can't believe you just did that. I mean..." The General began to swallow loudly, taking two steps toward the window. "I think I'm going to be sick."

Riddel, still holding the brain, sneered hatefully. "Stop the hysterical whimper this instant! What are you, the Head of Neurosurgery or some menstruating mouse? Get over here and cut the fucking spinal cord, or I'll have you busted to private."

General Weiss turned back around to face the Captain. He shrugged his shoulders as he tried to brace himself.

"I can court martial you. You'll be facing a full firing squad. Who'll shred everything from your quivering toes to your atrophied testicles," warned Riddel. "We're under the direct orders of the President of the United States."

The General came back over, grabbing the scissors with trembling hands. "Now cut, you bumbling spastic," Riddel ordered.

General Weiss did as directed, taking two full cuts across the thick spinal cord attachment. He bore down with the large dissection scissors, closing them each time with a grunt.

"Keep going. Here she comes!" the Captain cried out as he twisted the base. "You finally got it, mate. Oh, yeah. She's a heavy son of a bitch."

Riddel lifted the huge mass of severed brains up triumphantly. Then he carried it over to the area of the canister. Three large pieces of cut neural tissue flopped down onto the floor, one landing over the side lapel and shoulder epaulet of Riddel's jacket.

"Take off the damn lid." Riddel pointed angrily with his chin. "What are you? Completely unconscious?"

As the General lifted the cover, Riddel dropped the watermelon-sized mass into the round basket. The tissue fell with a loud thud.

Riddel wheeled back around, going to one knee as he stared at the floor, agonized. "So, could you tell me, shit for brains, how the hell did my jacket get back here?"

The General had walked over to the window and was now bent over in a gagging position. He still held a small piece of nervous tissue. He rose and faced the younger man defiantly. "Probably slipped under what you're treating as a carcass, you madman."

"Officers, we're above the site. Preparing to land," called the pilot.

The Captain signaled the pilot by flicking his thumb towards his feet. "Yeah, take it down, pilot."

He picked up his jacket as globs of tissue rolled off onto the floor. "Get those damn pieces into the canister, damn you. I can't believe my jacket's completely ruined!" The Captain disgustedly threw his jacket into the corner, while the General placed his specimen into the canister. "Shit."

Quickly, Riddel lay the body flat on its back, and hyper-extended the neck on the corpse. "Let's try to get the fragment out of his throat. Come on, General. I still need you to help dissect out the shrapnel."

The General slowly walked over, his face ashen, his eyes hollow. He then bent over, shaking noticeably as he gathered his pick-ups and the smaller scissors he had begun with. He knelt in front of the neck wound.

The General froze. "What could my fearless fart be doing now? Choking up again?" Riddel elbowed him away. Then he swept two of his fingers from each hand into the central wound at the neck. His fingers disappeared into the throat hole, as he grabbed blindly at the gritty material below.

He came up with a large section of trachea and esophagus, a ball of tissue approximately the size of three grapes. He inspected it, rubbing it between his fingers. "Shit! No lead. Nothing metal." He threw the material into the cannister.

"Well, we'll see what's in there a whole lot better when we get the body under fluoro. Okay."

The ambulance set down, a small jolt going through the back of the cabin. "Let's zip the bag up. Let's go. Help me, General!"

"All secure," said the pilot, looking into the back. The Co-pilot opened the back door and threw out the ladder.

The General stood frozen. His hips turned away from the body. He looked down with a shudder; his heaving back reflecting his stifled sobs. "What about the sheet?"

"You can forget that clot caked rag. It's ruined. Along with my dress field jacket." Riddel knelt down and zipped the body bag. Then he started to push the shoulders of the body toward the sliding door. The Co-pilot and a couple of agents moved over to help. "Aah, I'll just put in for a new one under a combat pay requisite. Say, it got my pants, also."

The Captain looked up to see the pilot and two of the ground troops coming into the back area to join the three others. He stood, pointing at the body bag.

"Okay, men. You can take it out." They began to drag it forward. "Hey, be careful with those remains, you idiots. You have the President of the United States in your hands. Show a little respect. Okay, let's get going."

The group removed the body bag. He and the General stood in the now empty back of the helicopter.

General Weiss turned hatefully to him, his eyes searing. "You're the craziest butcher I've ever seen." The General then began to sob openly. "I can't believe they put you in charge of this unit. You're an absolute maniac."

Captain Riddel reared up in total astonishment mixed with rage.

"Insubordination, General?" His voice rose instantly, becoming jagged and piercing. It became a shout, reverberating against the helicopter walls. "Get it the fuck under control, or I'll have you shot on this very spot. We still need you. You've got lots more dissecting to do."

The General took a half step back. "I absolutely refuse." The surgeon shook his head emphatically. "I will not do one more thing to help you." He wiped his eyes. "When I was asked to join this medical team three months ago, it was to work on mercenary troops. Suddenly, I find myself tricked into becoming part of an monsterous conspiracy. We're destroying evidence. Some of the people in charge knew what was going to happen. Because they helped plan it. And we've been put here so they can escape judgment. I can't rationalize helping in any of this."

"Robert Kennedy ordered our special team to be formed. Think he was plotting to have his own brother killed? You sound insane."

"Then he was tricked, too." The General shook his shaggy head. "I simple can't continue mutilating this wonderful man's body. I'm calling General Clark. He's in charge of everybody. Even you."

"Call whoever the fuck you want!" Capt. Riddel spat down on the floor in front of the General. Then he took two steps over to the ladder. He looked up menacingly. "I'm making out a report also." Riddel's eyes pierced the weak old man, who finally lowered his head. "We'll see who they believe." He took two steps downward. "You do know your career is finished. Kaput. Dead and buried."

Riddell climbed down the ladder. When his feet hit the soft gravel, he began trotting over to the men surrounding the body. They had already lifted it onto a gurney and were standing at attention.

"Okay, good job, men. Let's wheel it into the main autopsy room. And hurry. We've only got," He looked at his watch, beginning to shiver as he stood, sweaty and just wearing his shirt. "Shit, twenty-five minutes, thirty tops. Let's go." He clapped loudly. "Run."

The five men began running down the path. They lifted the gurney in the lowest middle path area where there were benches. They continued to guide it along. Then, they disappeared through the side door. The Captain looked furiously back at the helicopter. No one.

As he walked to the Hospital, he thought. 'Fuck that chicken-shit Commie traitor, anyhow. Sure wasn't any help. Shit, much more of a hindrance. And I still have to rebuild the entire right half of the skull. And give him a new ear. Well, the civilian autopsy tech that flew in on Air Force Two should have that completed by now.'

The Captain opened the right side door to the five-story brick building. 'Hopefully, the plastic surgeon will be lot more on the ball than this crumbling yo-yo. Better be. Shit, I can't do everything. And the command from Crown was already saying three bullets from the rear. Well, he'd give them what they wanted. Even if he had to cut off a brand new head and pin it onto the former president's trunk.'

CHAPTER SEVEN

Riddel opened the swinging door to the main autopsy room of Walter Reed Army Hospital. The body bag had already been slung on the floor and the body of the President lay on it's back on the cadaver table. Three enlisted men stood at attention near the foot.

Colonel Edwards, a board certified plastic surgeon, Chief of the Plastic and Reconstruction Wing of Eisenhower Hospital in Augusta, Georgia stepped forward. He saluted giving a warm smile. He was a dapper man, slender, short, mid fifties. He was obviously in excellent shape and his uniform was perfectly ironed. Riddel noticed things like that. He also had on an apron and gloves, which was even better.

"Greetings, Captain Riddel. Reporting for duty. Don't think we've ever met, but I've read all your directives." Edwards nodded his head. "Very thorough. In case you've forgotten, I'm in Plastics."

"Relax, Colonel. You've got a lot of work to do. Especially around the head and neck area. So did you look at the wound at the top of the forehead? What are we going to do with that?"

"I did." The plastic surgeon scanned the head area, shaking his head. "Now let's see." He put his gloved finger into the entry wound above the eye. "We'll have to use bone wax to fill this hole. Probably spread some fine cadaver wax on top. The autopsy tech from Dallas has just about finished shaping us an ear." The tech, in casual shirt and jeans, was bent over a side table. He turned, holding up the wax ear. "Then I'll swing a scalp flap to help cover things up. Spread some more wax. And we'll see what we have."

"Then that's what we'll do, by George, by the book. We just need a couple of pictures." Riddel looked around nervously. "Where the hell's the photographer?"

"Present, sir." One of the enlisted men in the back saluted sharply. Two cameras with flashes hung from his neck.

Riddel stalked over. "Get one of those fucking cameras in your hands. Now, soldier. We need you at full ready."

He snapped his fingers at one of the other enlisted men. "You. Go back to the helicopter and retrieve the brown plastic basket. It contains several small specimens. We've already begun the dissection in the helicopter." The enlisted man ran out, grabbing a leather jacket from the hook.

Riddel looked around again. "Where the hell is fluoro?"

One of the other enlisted men snapped a salute. "Present, sir." The soldier pointed to a large H-type frame in the far corner. "And there's the fluoro unit."

"Well, wheel it the hell over here, Sergeant. Aim it at the neck. And bring a damn leaded apron, damn you. Don't want to fry my nuts. Me 'n the old lady still got kids to think about."

Riddel put a lead apron on over his regular one and then donned his gloves. He leaned his head forward as the assistant x-ray tech helped him tie both apron strings in back. The senior x-ray tech wheeled the fluoro unit over to the body and aimed it as he had been directed.

"Turn it on, damn it," He yelled, moving over to the unit. "Hit the damn switch, someone."

The x-ray tech brought the pedal over to the Captain and knelt in front of him. "Here, sir. Just push down. You'll have better control."

"Thanks, Sergeant. Okay. Let's see what we got."

Riddel pushed the switch down. The circular green image was centered below at the top of the chest. "Shit, that's not his neck. But there's a hell of a fragment near T-4. Also, fractured the whole posterior rib. Should be an entrance shot near there, also." He paused, trying to guide the unit lower. "Uhm, could you move the unit down a tad, Sergeant?"

The tech did as directed. The image now centered clearly on multiple small radio dense fragments disbursed throughout the top of the fourth thoracic vertebrae.

"Wow. Kick me in the balls. Now how the hell are we going to get that out, without cutting open the whole damn body? Okay. Let's go up to the neck, damn it. We'll worry about that later."

The tech moved the machine head ward. The circular image now revealed two large fragments centered near the center of the neck wound. Riddel glared.

"Look at those two huge fragments. Grossly incompetent asshole General." Colonel Edwards came forward to look in the wound. Riddel took a half step back. "Not you but some idiot who's already off our team. As he should be. Anyhow, get me a clamp, someone. And get this fucking floro the hell out of here."

The tech wheeled the unit down to the foot of the table. Riddel took the clamp from the nurse and began to probe the wound.

"Can I give you a hand," offered the plastic surgeon. "Want some retractors in there, so you can see what you're doing a little better?"

"Tell me, Colonel." Riddel looked up from the wound, glaring. "Just what the hell is there to see?"

"The fragments, Captain." The Colonel had turned to the surgical table and pointed. "Sarge, get me a couple of Seine retractors. And a self-retainer. Give me a second, Captain." The Master Sergeant picked the instruments up from the table. Then, the surgeon took the instruments, and arranged the various retractors. He leaned in, then beckoned him over. "Come take a look." He touched the silvery metal objects with the tips of his small pick-ups. "There are your fragments. Want me to grab them up for you?"

Riddel nodded, trying to hide his surprise. "Now, that would be nice."

The surgeon bent over and brought the fragments out. He handed them over to Riddel. "Here's your bullets. Want me to initial them?"

"No, that won't be necessary." Riddel put the two fragments into a small plastic surgical specimen bottle, which he then placed in his front pants pocket. "Nice work. Say, Colonel. Could you excise the edges? Rather widely, mind you, so you get all the burnt skin borders out. Then close the wound. Quickly, please."

"No problem." The plastic surgeon nodded. "I'll have him closed properly in less than five minutes."

"Bless you, doctor. You don't know what a pleasure it is to work with someone who's not only competent but actually is trying to help me. I'm going up to the brain, now. If that's all right?"

"Great," the surgeon gestured with open hands. "I work better alone, anyway."

Riddel walked over to the head area and looked down. There were still fragments of brain and several tiny pieces of shrapnel at the base. 'Screw it. He got a head wound like this from something. Those small fragments could never be meant as evidence.'

Riddel moved up to the frontal area of the forehead and stared down in dismay. "Oh, blessed momma. Shit, what the hell am I going to do with this mess? What do you think, Colonel? Could you please take a quick look over here?"

The Colonel moved over to the right eye area. He pointed with a clamp. "You're going to have to excise these edges and close that hole in with bone wax. Put some cadaver wax over it as a base, then layer it all around to smooth it in. I'll be up to help you in a couple of minutes."

General Weiss walked in, his head bowed. The Colonel was the first to notice him.

"Hi, General. How you doing?" The Colonel waved. "Rich, it's me. Colonel Glen Edwards."

The General nodded. "Good to see you, Glen."

Riddel stood up and streaked over to the General. He stood directly in front of the General's nose. "Could you tell me what the fuck you're doing back here," Riddel snarled.

"Reporting for duty, sir. General Clark ordered me back. You're the high command on this duty. And I respect that."

"Now, General?" Riddel threw his hands up for emphasis. "But in the helicopter, where in the hell was that respect, then? You were totally insubordinate."

"I thought you were operating outside normal medical practice. I mean, you are still a doctor, aren't you?"

"You worthless son of a bitch! I want you out of my room, this instant." Riddel pushed General Weiss in the chest. "Before I drive a fucking osteotome through your bleeding heart, you asswipe."

"I can't do that, Captain, sir." The General shook his head, standing firmly. "I have to follow my superiors' orders. And they are to follow your direction until the mission is over. And Crown is completely satisfied."

"Amen! Well, at least you're starting to sound like a soldier." Riddel lowered his eyes in defeat. "Then get the hell over there, now. And take that stupid jacket off. Put on a damn apron and some gloves. You should know the drill by now, tough guy."

The Captain returned to the head wound. He took a scalpel from the tray and began excising the obviously burnt entrance wound above the eye and continuing into the temple area.

The soldier, wearing the fur-lined jacket, returned with the brown, rounded canister, "Where should I put this, sir?" Captain Riddel looked up, pointing to the corner. "Oh, almost forgot. I brought your jacket. Hung it up in the anteroom. Looks like it got a bit soiled, sir. Sorry. But it was already like that."

"Don't mention it again, wiseass." Riddel glared. "I told you to drop those specimens over there." He nodded toward the area of the corner. "So do it."

The soldier placed the canister against the wall.

General Weiss had handed his jacket to one of the enlisted men, then donned the apron and gloves as directed. He approached the table, standing in front of the Captain. "As commanded, sir."

"Better late than never." Riddel looked up with a sarcastic scowl. "I need you to take a look at the front skull area. Colonel Edwards suggested we build it up with bone wax. What do you think?"

"You're excising the frontal wound area, right?" the General bent over, studying the cranial vault.

"What the hell does it look like I'm doing? Of course," Riddel snapped, pointing to his dissection.

"Well, why don't you keep working on that part and I'll start on the skull wall," the General suggested. "That is my area of expertise."

"Yeah, hells, bells. Whatever, you fucking smart ass prick." He dropped his head, returning his focus to his dissection. "Just start doing something positive."

It took another five minutes for Riddel to fully excise the skin wound, continuing up into the scalp.

"Get me a specimen jar, please, nurse. Up here." Riddel dropped a rolled parchment of macerated skin into the jar.

Then he looked down to the neck area. The Colonel had just tied the running 5-0 suture at the edge of the neck wound. He cut the tail of the suture and applied a small xeroform dressing to the top. The plastic surgeon then turned to the Captain. "Can I be of further help, Captain?"

"Absolutely. Could you build him up a new front forehead? And how the hell are we going to give him a new eyebrow?"

"With an eyebrow pencil," Edwards suggested, giving a small smile. "Same way half the women in America do it. But first, we have to smooth everything out around the brow. So it looks natural." His hands began smoothing the wax.

"Alright, that's the ticket." Riddel patted Colonel Edwards on his hand. "You, at least, know what you're doing. I'll go help the General who's not as fortunate."

He moved two steps up to stand on the opposite side of the General, looking down into the cranial vault. "How's it going up here?"

"I've excised all of the fragments." The General glanced up at him. "And I've started building the skull area back."

"Good. Now where the hell is that?" Riddel leaned forward to better see the four-inch thick layer of bone wax laid down over the orbit. He turned his head slowly to stare at the General, his anger returning. "And that's it?"

"Well, Captain." The General returned his icy stare. "Your previous traction on the optic nerve plus, of course, the original major trauma had created a free floating eyeball. I had to resecure it."

Colonel Edwards had just laid down a huge amount of cadaver wax over the entire forehead. He deftly began smoothing the area down around the brow, using his thumb and a small rounded instrument.

Riddel studied the frontal area. "That looks great, Colonel. Pencil in your brow and let's get a picture." He turned to the enlisted men and called out. "Photograph. We need a frontal shot, now. Where the hell's the towel from Bethesda Naval? We need that, now."

The Colonel did as directed as the young photographer came forward with his camera. One of the enlisted men threw a towel on the table.

Riddel took the large superior flap of scalp tissue, grabbing the edges with his forceps. He began pulling it forward and down to cover the temple hole. Then he took a step back to study the position. "Shit, his right eye looks lopsided. Can't you push it back out a little?"

"I'll try." The General put his finger into the area of the orbit around the nerve. "The whole area is pretty weak." He pushed forward, feeling the entire eye socket moving forward as the grating sound of bone moving onto other bone resounded through the room.

"Yeah, that's a whole lot better," Riddel exclaimed. "Okay, let's get a picture."

The three doctors took a step back and the cameraman snapped several pictures.

Riddel glared at the neck wound. "Take that dressing off, damn it."

The Colonel lifted the xeroform dressing off with a small delicate forceps.

"Shit," Riddel groaned. "The suture looks much too obvious. Can't we hide it, somehow?"

"Well, they did a 'trach' at Parkland. Can't we say they closed that wound there," suggested the Colonel.

"Of course, we can say any damn thing we have to make it make sense. But still... Hey, I've got an idea. How about laying some blood clot over the area? To make it look a little less prominent." Riddel looked at the Colonel for confirmation.

Colonel Edwards nodded, then picked up a large clot of tissue resting near the ear. He laid it on top of the sutured area. "Like this?"

"Oh, yeah," Riddel smiled approvingly. "That's much better. Okay, we'll need another few pictures."

Several flashes went off and he nodded. "Let's turn the head on its side so the Colonel can get to the ear."

They turned the chin to the side. There was still a fist-sized area of bone missing from the rear area of the skull, well behind the ear. Riddel whistled. "What the hell are we going to do with that?"

"Easy, enough" replied the plastic surgeon brightly. "We can use the skin flap to cover it."

He looked at the Colonel with confusion. "I don't quite understand."

Colonel Edwards grabbed the two edges of the superior scalp wound and brought them together on the top of the head. He then pulled them both up. "Like this." The traction had restored much of the normal appearance.

"Oh, wow! That looks great. Terrific idea, Colonel. But how are we going to secure it?"

"Skin staple gun, please, nurse? Give it to the General," Colonel Edwards ordered.

The young man handed the General a loaded skin stapler.

"Staple at the base, Tom," directed the Colonel.

General Weiss put two large staples through the top edges of the scalp wound. The Colonel then released his forceps, allowing the tissue to fall back down against the head. He then studied the area. "So what do you think?"

"Hell of a lot better," exclaimed Riddel happily. "Let's get another few pictures. Then we can look at the back wound." The three doctors stepped away from the table, allowing the photographer to shoot a few side shots.

"Give me some help, here, men. I want to check out the back wound." Riddel pushed the cadaver shoulder forward, about half way. He stared at the nurse. "Could you give us a hand, here, nurse? Instead of playing stone statue?"

All together, they managed to flop the upper body onto its side.

They studied the nickel sized burnt entry wound at the inner or vertebral border of the scapula, about two hand widths below his neck, almost mid chest.

"So what do you think?" Riddel asked.

"Well, it's definitely an entry wound," the Plastic Surgeon replied. Weiss and the nurse nodded.

"Yeah, I agree. Let's get another picture." He ordered.

The photographer came in and snapped a few pictures. Meanwhile, Captain Riddel went back to the tray and retrieved a large pair of curved Kelly clamps.

He came back over to the wound as the photographer finished up. He drove the tips down into the wound, working the edges upward. He tried several blind clampings, his thrust jogging the entire body forward.

The Colonel watched with astonishment.

"May I ask, Captain, just what are you trying to accomplish?"

"Well, I want to see if I can get the shrapnel out. Around the third and fourth thoracic vertebra. You saw those fragments on fluoro."

"I most certainly did," the Colonel replied calmly. "But you're altering the bullet track. How are they going to study the path?"

"Well, they're not. They can't." Riddel continued grasping at the wound. "We won't let them."

"We?" asked the General, shaking his head.

"Fine, then its just me. I am the one in command." Riddel tried two more attempts at snapping down on the fragments. "Shit!"

"Try squeezing the wound edges. Maybe you can milk it out," suggested the Colonel.

Captain Riddel began massaging the muscles around the opening. A large bullet fragment came sliding out of the oozing hole.

"That's it. Great," the Colonel praised.

The General picked the fragment up with his forceps. "Want me to mark it?"

"Nah, not necessary." Riddel shrugged. "We may even push it back in. But that's later. For right now, we want to maintain as much of the true body picture as possible."

General Weiss scanned the brutalized corpse in total astonishment. He nodded slowly. "Yes, sir. I can see that. Maintain the original wounds, as best we can."

"Don't be such a sarcastic prick," Riddel snapped, annoyed at this sudden return to his old attitude. "You didn't do such a bad job on the head. Don't start sliding down on my evaluation sheet again."

"Sonny, I don't give a damn about your evaluation." The General looked up at the ceiling, seething. "Can't you see how outrageous this is?"

Riddel came over the top of the shoulder area of the cadaver, his shirt pushing against the body's side. "Don't fucking start on me, again. We still have to build up the head. You can give me the 'Sermon on the Mount' later. After we have the photos in hand. "

"Fine, then let's get to it." General Weiss turned to the tray and took a large handful of bone wax, smearing it onto a tongue blade. "We'll build up the side wall.' He paused. "Say, can we use a metal screen? It'll give us some foundation to build on."

"But that'll show on x-ray," Riddel wavered. "Shit, that was almost a good idea."

"We could take a couple of films off the fluoro," the General suggested. "Right now. Then we can use it and no one will notice."

Colonel Edwards winked at Riddel in agreement, who was thinking, 'or care' "Good thinking, General. For once I agree, completely. Okay." Riddel clapped his hands sharply. "You heard the General." He ordered in a booming voice. "Let's get an AP and lateral of the skull. Right now. Say, do any of you enlisted men have a lead shield anywhere around this shit hole?"

"In the corner," said the assistant tech. "I can wheel it over if you'd like."

"Of course, I'd like, Corporal. We want to shield two of the best damn surgeons in the whole United States Army, you idiot. Get it, ASAP."

CHAPTER EIGHT

The General and Colonel came over to the screen that had been set up slightly to the side of the body and stood behind it. Riddel looked around. Then he came walking over, and pushed between the two men. He put his arms around their shoulders, drawing them to him.

"Nice job, men. Really appreciate it." He nodded, smacking his lips in anticipation. "Bet the President gives us all commendations for this one." Riddel released his hug on the other two men. "Hey, what time is it, someone?"

"Seven oh six, sir," came the booming report from the photographer. "Want some pictures, now?"

"In a couple of seconds, son." Riddel waved his hand in the direction of the boy. "First we want to reinforce the front wall. But we're just about finished with the dissection. Thank the Lord. Come, take one of my star team. And me."

The photgrapher came over. Riddel gave a fierce smile as the General looked down at his shoes. The flash went off.

"All clear," called the x-ray tech. The Doctors stepped from behind the barrier and walked over to surround the head.

General Weiss slapped another huge tongue-blade full of freshly made bone cement against the steel mesh screen about the size of his hand. He began to smooth it out evenly. Then he repeated this procedure, coating even more cement onto the screen. He inspected it carefully, letting it set for about half a minute. The nurse was testing a piece from the basin, and he nodded.

"Okay, looks good. Let's put it in the front cranium." The General walked over to the wound with the prepared screen. Then he looked up at Riddel. "Can we remove the staples?"

"No, not both. Leave one, please." Riddel's eyes took on an imploring look. The whole reconstruction could fall apart. "Can't you put it in around the two? At least give it a try?"

Weiss agreed. "I can try."

"If we have to take one out, we will. But we don't want to disrupt the head anymore than we have to. So far, everything looks pretty decent from the surface." Riddel shook his head, agonized. "It's the most important area people will be looking at. They're already reporting a head wound."

"Oh, I see, sir," replied General Weiss coldly. "Well, we sure wouldn't want to alter the pathological specimen."

"'Sides, it's holding everything together." Riddel nudged the General in a gesture of friendliness. "We take 'em, we'll have his famous hair right back over his eyeballs. If we haven't pulled that right one out by now."

The General ignored him. "Okay, here goes." Weiss pushed the screen into the cavity and began to inch it forward. Finally satisfied with the fit, he compressed it against the side of his palm. He held it like that for over a minute. Then he tested it, pushing gently against the front temple area with his index finger. It held firm. "Looks good," the General proudly reported. Then he nodded. "Damn good. Okay, Glenn. Looks like you just have to attach the ear."

The civilian tech came forward with the wax ear. The Plastic Surgeon took it in both hands. Then, he attached the prosthesis over the raw, still bleeding stub, pressing down with gusto. Several heaping tongue blades of fine cadaver wax at the base were then worked in. He stepped back, admiring his work.

"Beautiful job, Glenn. OK," The General stared at The Captain. "If you want your pictures, I'd take them right now. We're running out of time."

"Okay, men. Wheel the floro unit out. Let's go." Riddel ordered loudly. He continued to appraise the body as the photographer now lurked. Several men wheeled the fluoro out of the room.

"Hold it, my man with the camera. First, wipe the damn head and trunk down," Riddel ordered. "Shit, looks like our cadaver just got hit with a fucking atomic bomb. Isn't there an irrigating system, anywhere?"

"Yes, sir. Here, sir." The Sergeant in command answered briskly. He brought over a large green hose attached to a six-foot tall tank. "The release is on the side, sir."

"No, you wash it down, Master Sergeant. Quickly." He ordered.

"Yes, sir." The Sergeant proceeded to wash the head and torso down of the larger clots and chunks of dead excised tissue, along with the old blood. Over a half a pound of macerated refuse soon lay on the drain guard by the corpse's feet.

Riddel surveyed the modified body with satisfaction. "Okay, let's get some pictures. Make sure you get the back of the head in a couple. Did you hear me, snapshot?" The photographer nodded in response. "And rotate that damn flap up when you do the back head shot. Cover up as much as you can." He pointed with his finger toward the base of the back scalp flap.

"Yes, sir," snapped the Master Sergeant. Two techs then descended on the body, placing it in various positions as the photographer walked around the head end, snapping rapidly. He took ten or more pictures in a matter of a minute.

Riddel stood in the corner, watching admiringly. Considering what he had been handed, he and his crew had managed some very impressive transformations in a very short period of time. With retouching and other photo tricks, it was looking all right. Command should be quite pleased. This exercise could turn out to be a real jewel on his record.

"Okay, let's get the body into the body bag. Is there a coffin around here?"

"Yes, sir. Standard metal shipping crate, sir," replied the Master Sergeant, referring to the mass casualty coffins used in evacuations.

"Well, get it over here. And put the body in that. Hey, and let's get going." Riddel checked the clock on the wall. "We're two minutes over right now. Do we have a recent fix on the Navy ambulance?"

"Yes, sir. Approaching off Wisconsin," reported the Master Sergeant.

"Okay, we'd better move it." Riddel started toward the door. "My staff and I will go to the helicopter, right now. Bring the body when it's properly secured." The Master Sergeant gave him a sharp salute.

The three medical men walked quickly to the helicopter, which was fully warmed up. As they were about to climb up the ladder, General Weiss continued to cast angry eyes in the direction of Riddel.

The body and the gray shipping casket arrived less than a minute after they had climbed up the ladder.

The helicopter ride over took less than six minutes. They could see the Navy ambulance and police entourage stuck behind traffic at the light on Cedar Lane. He surveyed the funeral procession through the back window and smiled. "Plenty of time."

The helicopter started to descend onto the lawn of Bethesda Naval Hospital, on the Old Georgetown Road side. "Should I use the landing pad, sir?" asked the pilot.

Riddel gazed out over the cold November landscape, looking onto Old Georgetown Rd. 'It was a very public stretch. Hell, there was a busy community hospital right across the street.' Riddel shook his head. "No, take it around back. Land near the rear corner of the parking lot. We'll move the body by ambulance over to the building," he replied, still looking out the window.

"Yes, sir," the pilot replied.

It took another few minutes to land the helicopter. The trio of officers got out of the helicopter first.

Colonel Edwards couldn't bring his hands up to his head fast enough to fend off the ferocious force of the rotors that continued to spin. "Damn,

I lost my hat," said the Colonel, watching it roll and float across the lawn.

"Hey, I screwed up a fitted dress jacket a while back. Five hundred bucks. So don't start complaining to me. But," Riddel paused for a second. "Nice work back there."

"Thanks. But I was only doing my job," said the Colonel stoically. "You want us inside for the formal autopsy?"

Riddel leaped forward. "By all means. I mean, I need all of my medical advisors around to help me. Got to bully the autopsy team. Keep them moving along." Riddel paused. "I think its Dr. Drune in charge. Real lightweight. He should be no sweat, believe me. We should have all the problem areas looking up to snuff within a couple of hours."

The General came over, listening to their conversation. "I thought it'd be something like that." They all began proceeding towards the building. The General reached the door first, and turned to face the others.

"Hey, you don't like me very much, do you?" Riddel asked, studying the grey-haired General's frozen manner.

"Actually, I don't think I've ever despised anyone near as much." General Weiss opened the door to the back of the hospital. "Today our President has suffered two monstrous crimes. But this one's far worse." Weiss took two steps into the entrance, then wheeled around. "I also want you to know, after tonight, I'm resigning."

"So do whatever the fuck you think you have to. Just one thing. Do it later." Riddel gave a sarcastic laugh. "Actually, I was going to suggest that very thing. Resign so we don't need a formal hearing to discharge your antique ass. But right now help us fix the body."

With Riddel leading, the trio of doctors entered the large anteroom. A table had already been set out with various snacks and refreshments. Coffee maker. Few bottles of liquor. The General took a seat, where he remained frozen down, refusing to remove his coat.

Captain Riddel and Colonel Edwards walked over to the table where they poured themselves some coffee.

A young soldier entered from the inside hall door. "Our apologies, officers. But there'll be at least a half-hour wait. The body is still in our Radiology Department. I'll keep you posted." He saluted and left.

About seven minutes later, he reappeared. He saluted again. "Our First Lady, Mrs. Kennedy has arrived with the official coffin. They have just passed the entrance gait." He left.

Three minutes later he reappeared. "The Honor Guard is presently carrying the bronze coffin containing President Kennedy's body to the Morgue."

Riddel leaped up and began running down the hall. He saw the procession stop in front of the area that served as the holding area. They were about to bring their burden into the autopsy room. He quickly intervened.

"Stop," he yelled, running down the hall to meet them. "Just put that damn thing against the wall. Well, for now, anyway. We'll need it later." Riddel pointed to the spot next to the door. "Then, you're dismissed."

They lowered the coffin in the corner, saluted, and left. There seemed to be two with quizzical looks on their immature faces. 'Oh, yeah,' Capt. Riddel thought. 'I'm just about ready to start explaining things to those enlisted toads.' Then Riddel entered the Autopsy Suite.

CHAPTER NINE

A slightly unkempt, decidedly ruffled doctor wearing a regular winter officer's uniform and long white lab coat came forward to shake his hand. They were both standing near the empty autopsy table.

"Captain Riddel, I'm Colonel Drune and I'm in charge of the autopsy. I understand you're Head Commander." Drune was a middle-of the road man in his late fifties, balding with large jowls. Two large tracts of bald space on the sides stopped at the top of his head. Red flaky scabs in several areas. Dull, nervous eyes. Frail build. Looking decidedly out of sorts with his acute position. This should be quite helpful when Riddel lowered the boom. And he definitely didn't want to wait very long.

"Yes, I am," replied Riddel, firmly shaking Drune's hand. "Glad to meet you, Dr. Drune. Yes, I understand we'll be in together on this thing. Do hope you know how to follow orders better than that General from Reed. What the hell's that bozo's name? Anyhow, that dimwit dummy just destroyed his entire career, in a matter of less than an hour." He pointed with his index finger. "Hope you don't wind up making that same mistake. 'Cause there's no second changes here. Not with matters of national security."

"We should be able to get started in half an hour or less. Why, X-ray's one of our very best departments." Drune shook his head in admiration. "Heck, some of those techs are just terrific."

Drune seemed a little off, unable to concentrate on his warning. 'Great. This could get ugly fast'. "Sure, Colonel." Riddel studied Drune carefully. "Look, you are aware of the true purpose of this mission. Right?" Drune gave a slow smile, then nodded. "So tell me, what do you think it is."

"To perform a complete autopsy on the body of our beloved President. So the perpetrators can be punished at a fair trial. Where this autopsy will prove to be key evidence, of course." The Colonel looked to him for confirmation. "Did I miss something?"

"Everything. Is there a private office?" He nodded solemnly. "Where we can discuss some top secret matters."

Drune ushered Riddel into a small back office. There was a small table and three chairs. A loveseat type couch with Scotch plaid fabric and blonde wood sat in the corner.

"Better sit down, Colonel Drune. Over there on the sofa." Riddel paced back and forth as the Colonel nervously crossed over to the sofa. When, the insecure man finally sat, he pounced. "There's only one reason this autopsy's being performed. And that's to prevent World War Three." He retrieved his top secret code plan from his briefcase and handed it to Drune. "Months ago, Attorney General Robert Kennedy created a special medical team to be stationed out of Walter Reed. Part of Project Freedom. This team consisted of skilled surgeons with the capability to alter bodies, in order to change evidence. Make it look one way, even though it may have happened altogether differently. Are you following me? The Kennedy's and their military staff at the Pentagon thought it was extremely important for national security to have my team on permanent ready."

From his briefcase, he now took out a piece of paper with the date November 22, 1963 printed at the top. He showed it to Drune but still held it in his hand. "This is from President Lyndon Johnson, our duly appointed leader as per the Constitution of the United States. Expresses the fact that I'm in charge of this autopsy. A Secret Service agent who was on board Air Force One handed it to me. I've trained for years to lead this mission. And as of two hours ago, there's only one purpose. That's to show that our late President was killed by one rifle fired by one shooter from the rear Book Depository. He fired three or four shots. We'll have to coordinate that part with Connelly's doctors, later. But that's not important. What is important is that President Johnson has ordered us to execute Plan B of Project Freedom. Subheading Foreign Assassinations. I've been in charge from the second we got the body. Are you starting to understand, now?"

"Yes, Captain," Colonel Drune nodded. "But how... "

"Don't think. I'll take care of everything. Me and my advisors." Riddel gave him a confident smile. "Just listen to us and it'll be fine."

The Colonel started to fumble about. "I really don't know what to say."

"Yeah, well, don't start worrying about it. See, that fancy coffin's empty. We've made most of the changes already." Riddel gave a quick, cocky laugh. "You've just got to tighten things up a little more. Make it look acceptable to all our loyal citizens."

"I don't know what to say." Drune continued to stand in the same spot, now staring at his feet.

"Shit," Riddel flared. "And, I thought all the morons were in the Army." He looked at his watch. Seven thirty. "Come with me, before I start calling you out."

Riddel pushed the morgue door open and walked back across the hall to the phone. He lifted the receiver and dialed the operator. The empty State coffin lay beneath it on the floor.

"White House, please. This is Captain Riddel. I need to speak to General Clark."

There was a pause of about a minute as he fidgeted with the phone. Drune closed the morgue door and looked up at him. "He's in with the President. They're getting him out."

Riddel stiffened as he brought the phone closer to his ear. He began a pacing journey down the hallway limited by the length of the phone line. "Yes, General Clark. This is Captain Riddel, Commander of Plan B."

"Yes, Captain," came the somewhat static reply. "We're keeping constant tabs. Look, it's vital to make that head wound look like it was inflicted from the rear."

"Well, I have to tell you. It was difficult enough covering up the front of the head." Riddel sighed into the mouth piece as he turned back toward the corner. "Where the entry wound was."

"Yes, Captain," Clark snapped impatiently. "But that's only half the job. You do understand that? We need at least two bullet wounds from the rear. We can save the other one for Connelly. The point is we need to have the visual proof to convince the public all the bullets were fired from the rear of the President. Are we crystal clear on that, Captain?"

"Yes, sir. Absolutely. I understand, sir." Riddel paced into the corner, then froze. General Clark was saying it like it was the easiest thing in the world to accomplish. "But how exactly do you propose I do that?" He slid his feet back and forth, then put one shoe up on the lacquered coffin. "See, I'm still a little unclear as to that one point."

"Well," came Clark's gruff reply. "He has some wound in the back of his head, doesn't he?"

"Sir, to be honest. He has no back of his head left." Riddel sat heavily down on the coffin, shaking his head. "The head shot was completely devastating."

"Then make it look like an entry wound. Make a new one if you have to. We don't care. Just get us some decent pictures. Now, son. Understand?" The fierce voice at the other end of the line seemed to be getting more and more agitated.

"Believe me, I'll try, sir. Some of the ones that we took at Walter Reed should be very good," Riddel replied, trying to sound upbeat.

"Yeah, but we need that rear entry wound, you stupid bastard. Don't make me say it again. Or I'll get you by your gonads, boy." The General was almost shouting. "And squeeze 'em down."

"I understand completely, General. Over and out." Capt. Riddel stood, pushing off against the fancy hand railing. "Oh, wait... Please extend my condolences to President Johnson."

"Just do a decent job." The General's newly hoarse voice replied. "Doesn't have to be brilliant, just decent. Okay? Call me later. Let me know how everything's coming along." The phone slammed down, shocking his eardrum.

Riddel returned the phone receiver back to its holder. He lifted his head, then wheeled around to face Drune. "We need a scalpel. And a bovi set up." He began to scream. "Stat. And I need the body."

"Yes, sir. But..."

"We have to create a bullet hole in the rear scalp. Presidential orders." He stared at Drune impatiently. "So where the hell's our body, you pathetic excuse for an officer?"

Drune began to shake. He looked down the hall and shrugged. "Probably still in x-ray."

"Well, let's get everyone the hell out of that room, right now." Riddel rolled up his shirt sleeves. "We can work down there."

"Yes, of course. Whatever you say." Colonel Drune turned to one of his orderlies. "Corporal, see that Captain Riddel's requests are carried out. On the double, Corporal."

Ten minutes later he and Drune entered the x-ray room. A young Sergeant guarded the door. An x-ray technician and his assistant were lifting several large x-ray plates out from under the x-ray holder fixed below the level of the table.

"Okay, men. Got everything you need," Riddel asked.

"Yes, sir." The head tech saluted sharply. "All that was ordered, sir."

"Good," he smiled. "Now get the hell out of here. The Colonel and I have some very important business to attend to. This instant. Move it, soldiers."

"Yes, sir." The two men ran out the door.

Riddel followed, poking his head outside. "Sergeant, make sure no one enters. Absolutely no one. Do you understand that?" He leaned into the face of the blonde, muscular soldier on guard at the door.

"Sir, yes sir." The soldier snapped.

"Good. We'll be about ten minutes." Riddel closed the door. Then, he locked it.

He turned to the body, walking over. The body lay on the table under a thin khaki colored sheet. "Shit, we have to turn him over."

"Oh, of couse. Well, I can call some of the enlisted men back, if you'd like," Drune suggested, coming over.

"Absolutely not! No more witnesses." He studied the body. "Hell, maybe we can just turn him on his side. I just need to get to the back of the scalp flap. Here, help me, Colonel."

The Colonel went over and they pushed the now increasingly stiff right arm of the body across the table, pulling the head onto its side. The body flopped over, revealing the back of the head.

"There," Riddel exclaimed happily. "That's fine. I can get to it from here. Now what instrument do you think I should use?" Drune looked lost. "To make the bullet hole wound in the rear?"

Drune continued this stunned look, like a deer staring into the headlights of a half-track. "I really don't know what to say."

"Is that all the fuck you can ever say. You sound like a babbling imbecile." Riddel snapped. 'He was going to be no help at all. Christ, I bet he hadn't been near a patient in twenty years.'

"Captain," Drune blanched. "I mean..."

"Look, shut your stupid pencil pushing mouth and try following orders. Did you get that scalpel I asked for?"

"Yes, sir." Drune pointed to a Mayo stand. "We have a full minor surgery set up, right over there."

"Well, roll the damn thing over, Colonel." He began tapping impatiently with his fingers. "Time's a wasting."

The Colonel wheeled the Mayo stand over. Then the Captain opened the large suture set. He grabbed a scalpel handle and slipped an eleven blade onto it. The extremely fine pointed tip glistened in the light.

He walked over to the back of the head and studied it. He wanted to make the hole low. He visually picked the midpoint. 'Bullet entered from bottom and exited out the top of his head. Right posterior. A third down from dead center.' He grabbed the flap of scalp and pulled it forcefully up to cover the gaping hole. "Here, hold this for me, Colonel." The Colonel did as directed.

"Helluva wound," the Colonel said, looking away.

Riddel drove the scalpel point down into the center of the scalp flap. He began turning the blade around, then pulled it out and inspected the hole. It was small but there was a definite opening. He turned back to the tray and grabbed a medium sized hemostat. He plunged the tips into the wound and then began spreading the curved back handles. The teeth spread out, tearing at the skin opening. 'The diameter of the hole seemed to double.'

"Great. This keeps looking better." Riddel threw the hemostat down on the tray. He looked around the room, quickly tensing. "Okay, got a bovi?"

"There's one in the corner." Again the frozen look. "But I don't think I know how to set it up." Drune began to walk to the back. "Should I call for the Master Sergeant?"

"Shit, you dumb fuck. What are you? A total cretin? You plug it in, for Christ's sake. What could be so difficult?"

Drune looked skyward. 'This guy really was an idiot.' "Well, I don't know where the wires or ground go. In the machine, I mean."

"Stupid shit! I can't fucking believe this? You're worse than incompetent. You're a menace. Okay, just let me think." Riddel pondered this for several seconds. 'Any sort of flame should be able to accomplish the look of burnt edges.' "Shit, we just need something to burn a hole with." He turned back to the Colonel. "Hey, you have a lighter? Or a book of matches? That should do it."

"Sorry." Drune almost hiccuped with nervousness. "I just stopped smoking."

Riddel pointed with a shaking finger to the outside door. "Get something from outside. Preferably a lighter. Stat, Colonel. Move your saggy stupid ass."

The Colonel, pale in the overhead red light of the adjoining x-ray developing room, opened the door. He went out. Less than a minute later, he returned with a zippo lighter.

"Give me that thing, you worthless slug." Riddel grabbed the lighter.

He moved back to the body. He placed the hemostat back in the wound and began heating the base of the instrument. There seemed to be no change. After less than a minute, Riddel pulled the hemostat out. "This fucking thing will take a fucking year and a day." He brought the wick over to the opening. "Let the head down, damn you. So I can center the flame."

Drune lowered the head and Riddel applied the flame directly to the hole. An acrid pungent odor began to emanate throughout the room, as the thick smell of burning flesh rose quickly.

He continued burning, going around the border twice. 'There seemed to be a good rim of charring in most spots.'

Then, Riddel pulled the lighter away and snapped it shut. He scrutinized his work carefully. There was a large burnt hole in the bottom area of the back scalp flap. Almost like a bullet hole. "Not bad. Hell of a lot better than before. Okay, get the body out. Let's start the damn autopsy." He looked at his watch. "Shit, it's going to be over one when we get out of here. Hell of a day."

Drune looked down at him with true fear. "I don't... I'm sure," Drune replied, correcting himself quickly.

CHAPTER TEN

The official autopsy began at eight o'clock sharp, civilian time. But it didn't truly get started until 2045, Army time. Drune and his first assistant hadn't performed an autopsy in many years and they were unfamiliar with the new mechanical autopsy table or x-ray/floro apparatus built beneath it, or the 16-mm. camera stationed above in the ceiling. They were unsure of just about everything. There were also about twenty men from various branches of the intelligence community packed inside, which added to the confusion. They milled in small groups, talking into their two-way radios. Top ranked Generals and Admirals. Lots of brass.

The second assistant, a true practicing pathologist from AFIP, arrived thirty minutes late which also contributed to the delay. Riddel fumed because from his interactions with Drune, he felt he would be a welcome addition. Actually a very necessary emergency addition. It was Captain Riddel, himself, who had ordered him brought in. Crown approved immediately. Shit, he needed someone around who was at least able to do something medical. So, this white tower med school Assistant Professor naturally took his own sweet time arriving from Virginia, of all places. Put just a little more pressure on Riddel's neck.

Finally, they started. They all inspected the ventral or abdominal side of the body for a full ten minutes, taking notes and drawing simple sketches. Walked around the head a lot, turned it around, looked inside the mouth, fingered the waxed area, then smoothed the material further. The entire scalp was being held together by the two #16 metal staples so they didn't go near that area. The true bullet hole in his temple was well covered with the wax, but still, close-up it was pretty obvious there had been an area of entrance.

There was surrounding swelling, hair and scalp missing or badly bruised in places at the hairline. The ear looked good, but it still was a wax ear, a prosthetic that looked dead, with no real color, hair, sweat ducts. Flat.

After awhile, they began to shift their attention to the neck wound. A perfect running 5-0 nylon suture held the huge transverse incision across the front. They sure weren't going to open it unless the Commanding Officer ordered it.

Drune walked over to Riddel, who was standing in the corner. "What happened in the neck area?" Drune seemed somewhat braced by his colleagues and staff around him.

"Tracheostomy done at Parkland. Sewed him up after they pulled the tube."

Drune's eyes opened wide in surprise. "It still looks quite large," he said, slowly releasing each word. He started back to the body carrying his metric ruler. "I've seen incisions for a goiterus thyroid that were smaller. What did they shoot him with, a 50 mm cannon?"

Riddel reached out and grabbed him by the shoulder. "Come on outside for a second, Colonel. I need to speak to you privately."

He escorted Drune outside, then turned to face him. "Better measure it smaller. A lot smaller. Take a couple of centimeters from each end." Drune responded with a bewildered look. "Hey, give the doctors at Parkland a little credit. Shit, you're going to make them look like real butchers. No one in their right mind will go to them for cold cuts."

Drune searched his commander's eyes uncomfortably. "Then what do we do with the head?"

"We say there's a bullet hole in the right occipital parietal area. An entry wound that blew the top of his head off." Riddel just needed to, no, wanted to strangle this man. He reared up. "What are you, a full bore microcephalic? What the fuck do you think we just did back there in the x-ray room? Now you go in there and point it out to everyone."

"But I'll have to pull the skin flap up." Drune looked utterly lost.

"So pull the damn flap up." He gestured with his palms to Drune, who reacted like he was a four year old being told there was no Santa Claus. "Who gives a shit?"

"But won't it look a tad suspicious?" Drune looked undecided. "All those observers present will witness me doing such an obvious maneuver. They're bound to report me."

"Listen carefully," he angrily slapped Drune's ear with the back portion of his hand. "You brainless piece of crap. The only people in there are agents. Secret Service, CIA, FBI, Naval Intelligence. But, they're all our people and they're all in on Plan B. They're not going to say anything because they know the game and the score. See, as part of our team they'll report exactly what you say. And far more important, what I say. Got it?"

"But still," Drune continued to look extremely hesitant. He took a half step back. "I just don't know what to say."

Riddel furiously put his hand over Drune's mouth. "Just don't say that again. Promise me you just won't say that again. Or, I'll have you shot right here in the hospital. Your widow will lose all her benefits. You'll have screwed up your family's future." He then patted Drune's shoulder, trying to settle down. "Now you go back in there as the Commander of the Bethesda Naval Hospital and the Head of the Department of Pathology. Hell, man, you're a damn board certified pathologist. And you will announce this damn exam the way we tell you to. Now, come on. No one with even three working neurons can be this stupid."

"Then, this isn't a proper autopsy," responded Colonel Drune indignantly.

Riddel looked up at the ceiling, seething. "No shit, Sherlock? You finally got it, you undiscovered genius. It's a total make up. The President of the United States is ordering us to do a makeover. And he's your Commander in Chief, as well as mine. So we'd better do it exactly the way he wants." He now reared himself directly into Drune's face, as his face reddened even more. "Or we're both completely screwed up the ass. Along with the nation. Want that on your conscience?"

"The President of the United States deserves a proper autopsy," Drune asserted tersely. "Especially after making the ultimate sacrifice for his country."

"Damn, you're almost making me cry. Big sloppy crocodile tears." He stopped, holding himself back from mocking Drune further. "Listen, he and his brother pulled lots of shady shit, themselves. 'Sides, last time I checked, he's dead. He's no longer President. What the fuck does he or his fancy-ass family care in the slightest what you say in some stupid report? One shooter or a hundred, ain't going to change his condition one iota. But far more important, we're alive and we have to follow orders from our new President. That Commander is being informed of what is going on in here up to this very minute. Do you want me to go over them with you, again? For perhaps the fifth friggen' time." Riddel put both hands around Drune's shoulders and shook him. "Or should I just call the White House? And end your pathetic career right here and now?"

Colonel Drune turned back to the door of the autopsy room, putting his right hand on the doorknob. Then his shoulders sagged, and his voice began quivering. "No, I'll go in and describe it the way you want me to."

"Okay, let's get rolling," Riddel replied with a clap of his hands. "We still haven't done the internal organs yet."

They moved back over to the autopsy table. Riddel went over to the chairs where the General and Colonel Edwards sat.

"Keep your eyes peeled on Drune." Riddel nodded contemptuously over at the Colonel. "Finally, he seems to get the point. But he's such a stumbling bureaucrat. Can't trust him for a second. OK, just watch things like hungry hawks eying a baby chick."

He left the two officers and moved closer to the table where the three doctors were working. He took a seat on one of the closest folding chairs.

Drune had entered and walked directly over to the corpsmen. "Turn the head to the left, please. I want to check the entry area." Several men in full white's jumped out and turned the head, including the shoulders, to the left side. "Pull up the flap, please, Pierre. Could you give me a hand?" Drune directed the practicing Pathologist. who picked up a pair of fine forceps. Together, they held the flap up. "This is the rear entry wound that most likely terminated the President's life." He pointed with his Adson's to Riddel's hole. Damn, it seemed to get lost in the matted hair. Drune stuck the distal teeth in, twirled them about. Lifted an edge. All the agents and brass seemed to collectively bend over and look in. Then, they began nodding, acting impressed, some taking notes, looking at each other, nodding again. As if that artificial small hole was something that could easily allow entrance of a missile causing such severe destruction to the back of the bony skull. This immediately became apparent once Drune and Pierre dropped the flap, which they now did.

Totally unbelievable to even Ridell, who felt himself cringe. Fortunately, not a stir from the audience. Not one government official was even slightly disturbed over the fact the President had suffered a severe area of damage with a large area of absent bone in the occipital area. Anybody could see it was bigger than a heavyweight's fist. Cracked bone all around it, radiating out like spokes. The bullet couldn't go through the skin tiny and then enlarge more than tenfold through the hard bone. Maybe they should have sutured the flap up. He was more than happy when Drune migrated to the throat.

Drune pointed with his forceps to the large neck wound. "There's obvious surgical alterations noted at the neck, which consist of a tracheostomy performed and sutured closed at Parkland Hospital. And, of course, in the superior area of the head."

Riddel almost dove out of his chair. He stood up, vigorously shaking his head. He finally got the Colonel's attention by snapping his fingers. He pointed to his own head, mouthing the words 'No surgery.'

Drune stared at him, trying to focus through his alternate pair of glasses. Riddel then made a forget it sign and sat back down.

"Okay, boys." Drune shrugged. "Let's turn the body completely over before we do the Rachatansky in the front."

Several enlisted men helped turn the body over. Colonel Drune walked over and pointed to the entry wound in the back. "There's an obvious gunshot entry wound on the right of the mid spine, in the area of the right thorax, at about mid scapula area." Drune used his gloves to smooth out the area. "Here, let's probe that." He then looked at the nurse. "Soft probe, please."

Drune took the instrument he was handed and slid the tip into the wound. After one three-centimeter probe, a bullet fragment came sliding out.

"And we have a bullet fragment in the subcutaneous tissue." Drune excitedly picked it up with his forceps and held it aloft to show everyone. "This may have come undone during the cardiac massage portion of the resuscitation attempt done at Parkland Hospital. Specimen jar, please."

The Colonel tossed the fragment into the plastic specimen jar handed him by the nurse.

Riddel stood, and began beckoning one of the senior Secret Service agents over to him.

"What's the matter, sir?" asked the middle aged over-weight man.

"Don't let him probe the wound anymore," Riddel whispered in the special agent's ear. "We may need it multidirectional for later. To explain the trajectory of the shots."

The Secret Service agent nodded. "I'll make sure he stops."

The agent then walked over and pulled Colonel Drune's elbow, whispering in his ear.

The Colonel dropped the probe back onto the tray, almost throwing it down in his haste. Then he continued with the autopsy. He jotted down notes in his own pad, along with dictating into the microphone that hung above him. This mike was connected to a highly sophisticated reel-to-reel recorder. The soft whirling sound of a 16-millimeter camera came from the small platform high above them.

Drune made the stem to stern anterior Y incision from the end of the clavicles to the symphysis pubis. He methodically went through each of the organs. He was unable to find a single other bullet fragment. The lung was up, meaning the back shot hadn't progressed very deeply. He pointed to the hyper inflated lungs. "Note the pulmonary membranes are intact. Punctures from posterior gunshot wounds often damage the lung in their travels." He smiled, pleased with his choice of words. He didn't even attempt to probe the back hole. Not now. He finally understood the game.

By the time Drune finished with the abdominal and chest dissections, it was past midnight. He did not, even one time, mention the fact that there was a huge laceration on the top of the President's scalp. Literally almost from the front to the back, caused by a massive explosion, from the rear, as he was postulating. Or from the front, as was the truth. And those two thick staples were holding it all together. He wasn't going to risk another assault by the Captain, who continued to eye him suspiciously.

A Secret Service agent entered the room. "Excuse me, doctors. But the widow Kennedy wanted to know how much longer before the body can be released. She's very tired."

Riddel quickly stood up. "Tell the former First Lady it'll be a while yet. Suggest she return to the White House. With all the extra studies necessary plus the embalming, we won't have the body ready," he shrugged, thinking. "Oh, until ten tomorrow morning at the earliest. After a loss like she's just suffered, she should go home and lie down. Get a little rest. She'll need her strength for the coming days."

"Yes, Captain." The Secret Service agent nodded. "I'll tell her just that." The agent then left the room.

About ten minutes later, Riddel could hear the police sirens in front of the building slowly fading as they drove onto Old Georgetown Road.

By one o'clock they had gathered specimens from all the various organs and weighed each. The large Rachatensky Y incision across the chest and abdomen was being sewed up by one of the techs using a large running #5 nylon suture.

He walked over to Colonel Drune and shook his hand. "Good job, Colonel. Happy to be able to report to Crown, you managed to come through in the end. Helped our team save our wonderful nation. I'm sure our leaders will be grateful for your part."

"Gee, thanks. That's very kind." Drune stopped, casting a nervous gaze. "So when do you think they'll want my final report?" Drune looked totally exhausted. "And what am I going to say?"

"Probably Sunday evening. And don't start worrying about any of your conclusions." He gave a sly laugh. "We'll write that up together. I'll call you about ten or so tomorrow. So be home. A lot easier that way." He gave Drune a conspiratorial wink. "And much safer, you understand."

"I'd still very much like to write up my own report," Drune responded indignant. "It would help me in my over all understanding. I'm sure later on they're going to be asking me some pretty pointed questions. I mean about the pertinent findings and all."

"I agree. But I wouldn't give it a thought. Hell, you'll handle that stuff like water off a duck's back." Riddel shook his head, trying to hide his complete astonishment at Drune's naiveté. "See, it's really quite simple. You don't remember shit. It was a very confusing time."

"I'll say." The Colonel smiled for the first time all night.

"Well, go get some sleep." He patted Drune on the shoulder. "We'll need you clear headed for tomorrow. So we can start putting the final touches on things."

He watched as Colonel Drune slowly trudged down the wide corridor of the basement of Bethesda Naval Hospital.

CHAPTER ELEVEN

At 0700 sharp, Saturday morning, Riddel drove his two-door two year old Army Green Ford coupe through the front gate of the White House.

By 0730 he sat in a small conference room directly adjoining the Oval Office. Director Hall, Acting Chief of the CIA, sat next to General Clark, Chief of Operations at the Pentagon and Riddel's direct supervisor and commander. Another middle-aged man in a suit was introduced as the head of Secret Service, and he sat on Hall's other side. Riddel sat at the other end of the six-man rectangular table.

An enlisted man came in with a stack of over one hundred black and white photographs. He laid them down on the table and then walked back to the door.

"Is this all of them," asked Hall with a scowl.

"No, sir. There's two more rolls we're just developing. The ones taken after the autopsy. We should have them soon."

"Good." Clark nodded. "Have them brought in the second they arrive, Corporal." The Corporal saluted. "You can leave now. Lock the door on your way out."

"Sir, yes, sir." The Corporal saluted sharply, then exited as ordered.

Director Hall and General Clark began flipping through the photographs. They came to the frontal views of Kennedy's head. There were four of them, almost identical. Riddel got up and all four men leaned over the pictures, studying them carefully.

"These look great. You can't even see the damn entry wound." Clark looked at Riddel, smiling. "Nice job, Captain."

"Yeah, those are some of the first pictures we took." Riddel sighed. "Thank the Lord he had thick hair."

The phone rang. The General lifted the receiver. "Yes, this is General Clark." There was a long pause as Clark listened intently, becoming more anxious by the second. "Can't we have someone talk to him, this doctor?" Another pause. "Yes, I admit it might look unusual. But we're dealing with a matter of national security." Another pause. "Okay. We'll start working on it from this end. And keep me informed, damn it."

The General slammed the phone down and turned to the group. "We have a major problem. One of the ER docs at Parkland is scheduled to give a news conference at 0900, Dallas time. And he's going to say he did a tracheostomy over an entry gunshot wound in the neck. Can you believe that shit?"

"No, he won't," Hall gasped. "Can't we shut him up?"

"We're working on it. But he's already made a similar statement yesterday afternoon to the TV people." Clark shook his head, agonized. "Damn doctors think they know everything. Act close to Omnipotent. Don't check with anyone."

"Screw the chain of command." Hall now looked back at the pictures, then began to feverishly look through the stack. "Where the hell are the pictures of the neck wound?"

Riddel grabbed a handful of pictures from the bottom portion of the stack and began flipping through them at the same time. He came to several photos taken at Walter Reed. "These are probably the best. We can always say it was an exit wound."

"That's a great idea," exclaimed the Secret Service Chief loudly. "But from what entrance wound?"

"The one in the back. I made sure Drune didn't probe it during the autopsy." Riddel shrugged. "Who'll know?"

"Where the hell are those pictures?" asked Hall, looking about.

Riddel pulled several photos of the back wound out. In each, Colonel Drune's hand held a metric ruler against the body, its tip against the spinal protuberance. They all began to look at the photos.

There was a knock at the door.

"Yes, who is it?" asked the General.

"Director Hoover," came the gruff reply. "Open up."

The General walked over to the door and opened it.

J. Edgar Hoover, wearing a double breasted suit, stalked in. He was followed by a well-built taller man with silvery hair.

"You all know Agent Ethridge." Hoover smiled to the two senior men. "Shit, is there any coffee around here? Too damn early in the morning."

"On the back table, Edgar," replied Hall, pointing to the silver tray set up in the back.

Hoover walked over to the back and Ethridge prepared him a cup of coffee, making a show of dropping two lumps of sugar into it before handing it to his chief.

"Thanks, Parnell." Hoover grabbed the cup, then turned back to the table. "So how's it going?"

"Not too bad. There's just one problem that's come up." Clark took a deep breath. "But we're working on it."

Hoover sat, placing a napkin carefully down beneath the saucer. "And what is that?"

"We have the head wound covered. Single rear puncture wound in the back scalp, causing the entire right superior skull area to be shot away," Hall recited.

Hoover scanned the pictures of the skull area. "Okay, I can buy that. As will our fiercely faithful public. So what's the problem?"

"Well, we'll let Captain Riddel explain. He's the Commander of the Autopsy Team." Clark nodded to Riddel. "He's been with the body since the beginning."

"The throat wound is the problem, sir," Riddel stated gravely. "Some jackass ER doctor at Parkland is saying it was an entry wound."

"What the hell does he know?" Hoover looked up angrily. "Can't we refute him?"

"Of course, but we're still trying to explain what it was, instead," Riddel paused deliberately. "I came up with the idea of saying it was an exit wound." Hoover nodded in agreement. "But the problem area remains where did the bullet come from."

"From the sixth floor book depository window, you fool. We have three shots from the rear. One obviously hit Connelly. That's easy. One struck the President in the back of the head. That's easy, also." Hoover became silent, obviously deep in thought.

"And the third struck the body in the mid back chest area and exited out the neck," continued Riddel.

Hall, Clark, the Secret Service Chief, Ethridge and Hoover all nodded, then looked at each other.

"So what's the problem?" asked Hoover, finally.

"Well, sir. The wound in the back is really low down. The trajectory is wrong." Riddel opened his hands, as he swallowed hesitantly. "Some people might not believe it could actually happen that way."

"Put the pictures of the back wound up on the board." Hoover barked. "Let's study them."

Riddel did as directed, tagging four pictures on a large cork board. They all came over and studied each picture.

"Shit, I can see what you mean," replied Clark, squinting over. "Any ideas?"

"Well, sir, I've been thinking about that. And, that is if you and the other Commanders agree, well... We can always give him another entry wound, up higher, nearer the neck." Riddel held his breath, waiting for their response.

"Why that's a wonderful idea," replied Clark, going over to the drawing board. He quickly sketched the lateral form of a man on the paper with his pen. Then he grabbed a large black magic marker. "The bullet entered, oh..." He began to hunt about, going slowly up the body from the actual true mid thorax wound. "Oh, up around here," the General pointed to the trapezius border of the neck. "And it went out, here." He then pointed to the throat.

"That makes sense," said Hoover, relaxing noticeably. He walked back to the table and brought his cup of coffee daintily to his mouth. "So what's the problem? Go do it."

"Yes, sir," Riddel saluted. "I'll have to get back to the hospital. And I'll need some things in order to do the alterations."

Hoover walked over and faced Riddel, his foul cigar breath very apparent. "So what the hell's the problem?"

Riddel cowered under the shorter man's burning gaze. "Well, I'll have to call Colonel

Drune and get him over there to join me." Riddel looked up to the ceiling, deep in thought. "And we'll need a photographer, of course."

"I'll take care of all that right now. Anything else you need?" Clark lifted the phone at the table.

"No, that's about all. That'll be extremely helpful. Drune's so stupid, he's gone into a panic about three times already." Riddel shook his head. "Say, do any of you gentlemen have a lighter I can borrow?"

"There's no smoking in here, Captain." Hoover coughed, bringing up some phlegm which he spit into a paper napkin. Then he gave a sinister smile. "Bad for your health."

"I need it to make the new entry wound look more natural." Riddel reported.

"Captain", Hoover put his cup down heavily. "Frankly, you can explode a napalm canister in it, if it'll make the wound look any better." He went to the board. Taking the four pictures of the back wound off the bulletin board, the FBI

Chief flipped open a Zippo and lit the photos. Then he threw them, still burning, into the round garbage can.

"I'll have my car drive you over to the hospital." Clark volunteered. "It'll pick you up off the back right side entrance. I'm getting Drune on the phone now. We'll have it all covered."

"Make sure you do, Captain. The President of the United States will not be pleased if we have a problem." Hoover then spit into his own handkerchief. He began to fold it over deliberately. "Too much news attention already. Making that drug-addicted wanton degenerate into a cock-sucking saint. If that don't beat all." Hoover sat down, his heavy frame causing the chair to creak. "I'll never understand the unending stupidity of our well educated citizens. Hayseeds will swallow any bucket of unadulterated horseshit we throw." Hoover put the handkerchief back in his rear pocket. Then he held the lighter up and Riddel took it. "No matter how ridiculous it seems to anyone with even a pinch of old fashioned common sense."

The phone rang. Clark picked it up. "Yes, have him driven to the right rear entrance, thank you." Clark then hung the phone up. He stared directly at Riddel. "So what the hell are you hanging around here for? You've got a job to do. Get going, Captain. Call when it's over. And the Director wants his lighter back by Monday."

Riddel saluted the group, then walked slowly to the door. As he opened it, he heard Clark say, "Giancana's man Rosselli has arrived."

"Excellent," replied Hoover's unmistakably gravelly voice from the back. "He'd better silence the pigeon, and fast. Damn Tippit. And that psycho White. They were your men, Commander." Riddel stepped out as the door began to swing closed. "Oh, and make sure you replace the windshield on the limo. Not good leaving that piece of evidence hanging around." The door closed and Riddel could hear nothing more.

The ride back to the hospital was uneventful. Riddel sat in the back seat of the General's extra large sedan, nestled in the soft cushions. He had been sketching on a yellow pad, drawing a right side, a front and a back figure. Now, he began to draw various trajectories of bullet's entering from the rear. He'd drawn only three when the limo hit the south entrance of the Bethesda Naval Yard off Wisconsin.

The guard stopped them at the gate. He got out of his guard house and bent over the window. "Yes, sir?"

The driver immediately snapped to attention, stating, "Captain Riddel in the back. Autopsy Commander."

"Right through, sir," the guard said, running back to the guard house. He pushed the button to the wood guard, which began rising almost immediately. He came back out of the hut. "Commander Drune is already waiting on the

Captain, sir." He snapped to attention. The car drove down the path.

Riddel met Colonel Drune in the morgue area. He was dressed in greens and wearing his white long coat. There were several enlisted men running around the body which had a sheet over it.

"Okay, all you men. You can get out now. The Colonel and I have to do some further studies. And lock the door when you leave."

The men ran out as directed. Riddel went over to the left hand and wrist of the body. He pulled off the sheet and let it fall to the ground. He donned his apron and gloves. Then he waited for Colonel Drune to do the same. He pulled the cadaver's wrist, turning the body on its side. "Here, Colonel. Hold him like this. This'll only take a second."

"Wow, the body really is stiffening up badly. And look at all the dependent rubor and petechia that have formed." Drune pointed with his gloved finger across the red and blue torso tatoos. "Isn't that going to show on any of the photographs?"

"Come on, Colonel. The photo lab can retouch them. Some of the head shots need work, anyway. Look, we don't have a fucking choice here." Riddel looked around the room. "Have you got that instrument tray?"

"Just the old one. From the procedure last evening," replied Drune.

"So, that'll be fine. What the hell's the difference?" Riddel asked indifferently.

Drune came forward, paling noticeably. "Well, it won't be sterile."

"Are you completely brain dead? The body's ready to decompose and now you're worried about some latent bacteria. Jesus Christ. I can't believe less than an hour ago I'm discussing alternate plans with Hoover and Hall and just about every other Chief from every service running our blessed country. And now I'm back here, trying to execute these very same plans with just about the sorriest stupidest most worthless excuse for an officer in the entire Armed Forces. Tell me life's fair."

Riddel went to the Mayo stand and took out the eleven scalpel blade. He held it up. "Good. Still loaded." Then he looked at the blood caking the entire surface of the blade with disgust. "Shit, do we have any peroxide? This blade looks like it's gone through a belly of feces." Drune shook his head, shrugging. Riddel glared, "Fuck it and fuck you, too."

Riddel went over to the body and drove the tip of the scalpel blade into the area of the right mid trapezius. Then he twisted the blade around viciously. He stared at the wound and went to his pocket. He took out the large Zippo lighter which he had obtained from Director Hoover. He flipped it open, then twirled the flint. Then Riddel proceeded to cook the area for over a minute.

"Boy, I hate that smell." Drune turned away.

"Stop your disgusting bitching, baby. We'll be done in less than a minute." Riddel reapplied the lighter for another thirty seconds. He moved the apex of the flame around the border a few times. "There. That's fine. Now, where is our dear photographer? All these ranking dignitaries from around the world are coming to pay their last respects. Which means we have to get this pain-in-the-ass body back to the White House just as soon as possible." Riddel snapped the lighter closed. "OK. Where's the nearest phone? I have to call the White House and tell them everything's been corrected."

"But what about my original autopsy notes?" Drune paused anxiously. "They show the bullet hole being much lower down."

"So burn them, Colonel. Write up some new notes. Who the hell will know?"

"Well, I really don't know what to say."

"Then don't try." Riddel gestured. "Get the hell over here and hold the ruler. Make sure it covers the lower hole. I'll get the damn photographer in. Better wrap this up before I make my call. Especially with a malignant disaster like you around to help me."

Five minutes later Riddel watched as the First Sergeant began to shoot a roll of film showing the recently created bullet hole in the right trapezius. He watched Drune as he clumsily moved about, switching locations around the body while continuing to hold his ridiculous ruler over the real bullet hole.

"Incompetent asshole." Riddel wheeled around. "Dumb son of a bitch," he mumbled under his breath as he walked over to one of the enlisted men. "Where's a private phone. I have to call the White House."

"You can use the Lieutenant Colonel's office if you'd like, Sir."

Riddel smiled for the first time that morning. "Yes, young man. That would be mighty fine."

The man led Riddel into the Lieutenant Colonel's large well furnished office. He waited until the enlisted man had saluted and left, closing the door. He locked it.

Then he lifted the phone. "Yes, this is Captain Riddel, Commander of the Autopsy Team.

Get me General Clark at the White House, immediately."

There was over a minute pause.

"Hello, Riddel, this is the General. How did it go?"

"I'm happy to report, everything went perfect," Riddel exhaled, still trembling. "Yeah, just about perfect."

"Wonderful news." There was a slight pause. Riddel could hear clapping and shouts of approval in the background. Then came the General's excited reply. "We're all elated. So when can we expect to have the films?"

"I can get the developed pictures to you in less than an hour. Do you want any larger than standard?"

"Not necessary. Eight by tens should be fine." General Clark's voice took on a more threatening tone. "If they show what we want, of course."

"Oh, that they will, I promise."

"Well, very good. Okay. We'll be back to you after we look at the photographs." General Clark paused, and Riddel could just manage to hear him say, "What was that, sir?" Then there was another pause. "Oh. And the President says to tell you, 'Good job, Captain Riddel.'"

"Really?" He almost dropped the phone. "Why that's wonderful. Oh, my God. Tell the President it was an honor and privilege to head this mission. A most noble exercise."

"I will," the General replied curtly. "Okay. If everything looks all right, get ready to cremate the body ASAP. In fact, go ahead and send the coffin over to the White House right now."

"And tell him I'm sorry about..." The phone slammed down. "his terribly tragic loss." Drune entered the room. Riddel placed the phone on the carriage, then looked up at him. "You won't believe this. After all our hard work, now they want us to burn the damn thing."

Drune shook his head. "Oh, I see. So, will they be needing the Bovi after all?"

"Hell, no. A furnace." He looked at Drune while he snapped to attention. "But our proud democracy has been saved." A beaming smile swept over his face, and he inhaled mightily. "And President Johnson realizes our vital contribution. Bit of a shame nobody else will. But, hell, man, that's the fucking military. We know what we accomplished and that's the important thing."

AUTHOR'S NOTE

The presidential autopsy scenes emanate from personal conversations with a friend and colleague, a trauma surgeon who in late 1963 was assigned to the Pathology Department of Bethesda Naval Hospital. This extremely honorable man was scheduled to perform the Kennedy autopsy, as he had performed all the autopsies during the month of November. This was his primary responsibility in this assigned rotation. The top brass did not get involved with what was considered clinical work, and had neither the recent experience nor technical ability to perform a skilled autopsy investigation. However, at the last moment, this young Naval officer was dismissed and sent home by government agents, at gun point. After much discussion with the enlisted men who were present at the autopsy, this doctor eventually came to understand several key things. There had been a special forensic team working out of Walter Reed Army Hospital who performed a preliminary operation on the cadaver before it arrived at Bethesda. They altered the remains in order to demonstrate bullet wounds coming from only one direction on JFK's body. Both the rear shots cited by the Warren Commission were artificially produced by this group of surgical and technical experts. The top secret squad had been training for months, specifically for this mission. The body was later destroyed as was a good deal of the other evidence.

MORE AUTHOR'S NOTES

Also of note, my e-mail is ezfriedel@gmail. com. I will gladly come speak before book clubs about my novel. Maybe we can split the travel costs? This is an extremely important topic which I'm obviously hooked on. All I request is you buy and read this piece and a few others, BEST EVIDENCE by David Litton, CONSPIRACY by Anthony Summers, DOUBLECROSS by Chuck Giancana, the Fetzner paperback on the inconsistencies in the Zapruder film, along with watching the History Channel series noted in the dedication. Then, basically caught up, we can start going forward. Science does win out in the end. Even if it does seem to be taking a very long time.

ABOUT THE AUTHOR

E.Z.Friedel is a board certified orthopedic surgeon who graduated from Albert Einstein and Mt.Sinai residency programs in New York. After serving as a major in the U.S. army, he moved to Montgomery County, Maryland where he began his private practice. He was the chairman of the Orthopedic Surgery Division at Washington Adventist Hospital for over ten years, specializing in sports medicine and trauma. He was a staff member at Suburban Hospital, across the street from Bethesda Naval Hospital, where the JFK autopsy had been performed. He was friends with the Naval Surgeon assigned to perform that autopsy. His many conversations with this doctor who went on to become the Head of Vascular Surgery at a nearby major hospital provided the first hand, true life account that has formed the basis for his novel. In another life, he was sports editor of his high school newspaper, the Valley Stream Crier.

As a baby boomer, Dr.Friedel has a special interest in biopics about the stars of the late 50's and early 60's. He has combined his knowledge of forensic medicine and psychiatry to write The Red Diary, a memoir based on the last years of Marilyn Monroe's life. The period leads up to her murder, with a scientific explanation of the massive cover-up that followed. The Regenerates is a much more lighthearted and sexy romp. A sports medicine physician falls in love with two women, while developing a method of regenerating super limbs. He performs this operation on several unlikely patients, who he then adds to the roster of a failing football team. The results are outlandish, yet inspiring. Roadside Unrest is a horror story about a roadside memorial tree with special powers. When a doctor moves his loving family into the model neighborhood and petitions for the tree's removal, all hell breaks loose.

Printed in the United States
76725LV00001B/50

9 781425 992163